GIFTED

CURSE

BOOK ONE OF THE CLOVEN PACK SERIES

D. FISCHER

1

A Gifted Curse (The Cloven Pack Series: Book One)

ASIN: B072631P5

ISBN-13: 978-1973890898
ISBN-10: 1973890895
BISAC: Fiction / Romance / Paranormal

To the ordinary who stumble
across their dreams . . .

Everything in this book is fictional. It is not based on true events, persons, or creatures that go bump in the night, no matter how much we wish it were…

CONTENTS

CHAPTER ONE

Makenna Goldwin

Click. Click. Click.

I stumble, flail my arms, and slam into a building's brick wall. "Fucking hell," I growl, wincing to the sting on my palms. I'm making my way down the sidewalk in these damn heels I insisted on purchasing for 'work related' purposes when my left heel gives out from under my foot. I glare accusingly at them. I shouldn't have boughten these death traps. They were over-priced and far too girly. Somehow, and definitely against my better judgement, I managed to convince myself that I needed them in order to be taken more seriously.

Letting out a stream of curses, I refuse to believe my ankles can't function right; this is entirely the shoe's fault. It is supposed to be like walking around on your tippy toes, right? But with more support? A growl escapes my lips and I shove away from the wall.

I steady myself with a quick glance around before I topple over for the world to see . . . again. Not that there are many people around. It is, after all, what some would call 'after hours.' The sidewalks are nearly abandoned, save for the guy who needs a belt and the group of police officers gathered by their cars.

Heels have never been my thing – I despise them. In order to maintain some kind of professionalism, though, I knew I would have to purchase something other than flip flops, sneakers, or slip on shoes. I doubt my clients, current or potential, will take me seriously if I interview them in my nice blouse and skirt accessorized by my running sneaks. Wearing these heels is bad enough, but this skirt is a whole other matter. I straighten my circus outfit and press on, waddling down the sidewalk.

I'm waiting for the day to come when it's appropriate to wear my beloved jeans, plain T-shirts, and flip flops to such interviews, but I have a feeling that's a long way coming. That may be considered appropriate when pigs fly.

Entering my destination, I'm instantly smacked with familiar, yet overpowering scents. I inhale deeply, wrinkle my nose, and take in my surroundings as the glass door closes behind me.

The police station reeks of coffee. I adore that dark delicious brew, but only a coffee drinker can tell when a coffee machine has been used one too many times without the privilege of being washed. That is certainly the case here. It's a shame. Truly.

7

Everything is white in various stages of shiny or dull. The walls, the tiling, the countertops – everything except for the men and women in blue that mill around completing their evening duties as law enforcement personal.

Despite the familiar scents, police stations always make my skin crawl. Whenever I'm in the presence of a police officer, I feel like I'm being judged for crimes I may or may not have committed. The look they give as someone passes them is like they're privy to all past unlawful sins. Not that I have a lot. Maybe a few stolen goods here and there for survival. It's the same feeling as driving past a police car and tapping the breaks regardless of the speed – heart stopping, palms sweating, the intense anxiety of never being completely certain that you weren't speeding even when the speedometer reads sixty-five.

I mentally check myself to make sure I'm not carrying any form of weapon. It wouldn't do to be tackled to the ground wearing heels and a skirt. The word 'undignified' comes to mind.

Looking straight ahead to the woman behind the front desk, I unsteadily make my way to her. I silently applaud myself for not face planting on the beautifully polished white floor.

"What can I do for you?" the woman asks in a bored tone, continuing to glance at the paperwork in front of her. She flips a page over and continues to read.

I wait for her to look up and meet my gaze, but she seems uninterested in my presence. I clear my throat, uncomfortable with her lack of manners.

"Makenna Goldwin, PI and Micro-Expression specialist. I'm here for Agent," I look at my hand where I had scribbled the name of the gentleman who had called me, "Johnson."

The receptionist slash police-woman finally looks up and gives me a once over. She's a brutish lady with short red hair streaked with grey, heavy wrinkles, and a developing mustache.

Not everyone buys the Micro-Expression specialist title or the profession. Some people categorize it right next to psychic crazy chick with a side of 'waste of time, resources, and money.' Fortunately, I make a living with the talents I have, so their judgment is moot.

I lean against the counter, pluck up a pen, and twirl it in my fingers. She glares and satisfaction fills me.

Law enforcement tends to not be friendly toward private investigators. I have no idea if it's a territorial thing and they feel as though we are pissing all over their marked trees, or if it's because sometimes we can make them look useless when we catch the bad guy. Meanwhile, they're busy with their required steps and checklists. I mentally shrug. Either way, I was called here for a job and I plan to do it.

Madam Mustache snatches my pen away with a snarl. My impatient fingers drum against the white counter, wordlessly letting the woman know I am waiting for her to take action and point me in the right direction. It's either that, or . . .

I eye another pen. "I can do this all night," I murmur sweetly.

Before my oh-so-friendly police officer friend has time to finish her mental assessment of me and inform Agent Johnson that I had arrived, we both glance to our right as a door opens.

My hand stops midway to another pen. *Sweet baby Jesus.*

Together, we watch as a very attractive, very large, burly man with short, cropped blond hair, slips gracefully through the door. I note that, amongst his extremely good looks, he isn't wearing a blue uniform. Instead, he wears an FBI badge pinned to a buttoned long sleeve shirt. His broad shoulders and impressive build fill out his clothes nicely, leaving nothing to the imagination.

I blink twice trying to clear my head of the sexual images that begin to surface. This must be my guy. Wait, no, not *my* guy, *the* guy. I clear my throat. I'm not ogling, I swear. I mentally chastise myself while every sensitive part of me begins to tingle. *Treacherous body.* Thank heavens my bra is padded. My nipples could cut glass right now.

Without giving another glance at the woman behind the desk, I walk right up to Agent Johnson and hold out my hand.

"Agent Johnson, I'm Makenna –"

He cuts me off with a dazzling white smile and shakes my hand. His fingers alone are larger than my palm. It's like I'm grasping a bear's paw. "Goldwin. I know. I recognize you from the picture on your social media page. Thanks for coming down. Please, call me Evo."

My word, the heat that travels from our joined hands all the way through my body is unnerving. Am I the only one who feels that? I must be, because his smile never wavers.

Nodding behind him, he leads me through the door and into a hallway. Wouldn't you know it – more white adorns the walls and floors. Is the color supposed to unnerve people? Because it's working.

"It's not a problem, Evo. I'm glad I can help. Our phone call was pretty brief. What is it, exactly, that you need my help with?"

Evo spares me a glance as we walk side by side. My heels click and echo in the hall, and I note with dismay that his shoes don't. The rubber of his sneakers squeak. I instantly don't like this man.

"We have a suspect in one of the interrogation rooms. I can't give you the full details. You aren't cleared for such information, but I can give you the basics of what I need from you."

I don't point out that I will probably hear my fair share of the information I'm not 'cleared for' during the interrogation. I'll let him worry about that later.

At my nod, he continues, stopping just outside one of the many doors. God only knows how he knew which one to stop at. They all look alike with no numbers. "A few missing women have come to our attention and the gentleman we are questioning today has been seen chatting with each missing person just before the time of their disappearance. What I need from you is to tell me anytime you believe he's lying or telling the truth. One-word answers will do fine. We can't have you in the interrogation, but I'll have you watch from the observation room. I'll have an earpiece in to hear anything you have to say." He points to his ear and sure enough, there is the telltale earpiece a typical FBI agent wears. How cliché. I wonder where I can get one of those. Perhaps Madam Mustache can help me out with that.

"The audio directs straight from the observation room's speaker into this earpiece. I don't know how you do what you do, but I've heard you come highly recommended." Evo nods as he finishes talking and opens the door for me to enter.

I nearly snort. Who the hell recommended me? I don't exactly broadcast my services. Mostly because I can't afford to buy business cards, posters, or advertising in the paper. That, and I have yet to nail a high-end client.

The tiny observation room contains a small desk with files flipped open. They're placed on a table in front of the one-way glass. Another female agent is waiting in the shadowed corner, and she engages Evo in a quiet conversation as soon as we're through the door.

I leave them to it. Wandering over to the small desk, I glance down at the papers, thumbing the corners. I'm a naturally curious person and can't help myself when things pique my interest. My eyes instantly fall on my picture paperclipped to the front – they have a file on me. Frowning, I read.

Makenna Goldwin, age twenty-seven, PI Specialist. My date of birth follows, which, technically, is just an estimate the doctors gave when I was found abandoned and brought to the hospital. My foster families are listed, as well as my educational background. Since I don't have much in the way of schooling, there isn't a whole hell of a lot listed. Shame colors my cheeks.

Just beneath that is a little history they've scraped up. It basically states I have no family, I've lived on my own since age sixteen, and I have no college education. It makes me sound like a loner. A very uneducated loner with no life. I suppose I am.

I peek over my shoulder as their whispering becomes heated. Sounds like the female agent doesn't want me here.

Having no family has always stung a little, but I've been alone for so long that I'm comfortable with it. I've learned to never rely on anyone, and I don't know if I'll ever be able to.

Some might say I have abandonment issues. I prefer to label it as self-preservation due to experience. If I got comfortable sharing my life with another, what would I do if they suddenly left? I'd be broken and left to pick up my pieces alone.

Putting myself in that situation would be asking for trouble I don't need in my life. I've had too much abandonment for one lifetime.

While thinking those thoughts, something inside me tells me I'm lying to myself. Something inside me craves comfort and safety in numbers. I mentally squash it down like a foot to a full trashcan.

That other 'something' often weighs in on my thoughts and actions. I refer to her as my alter ego because, in a sense, it's like a whole separate me. My alter ego and I don't always agree with each other. We have different views on life. She'll weigh in on my thoughts and actions and how I should handle situations. Her suggestions are based on primal instinct while mine are more civil with a touch of 'trial and error.' I'm aware of how abnormal this is, so I keep her tucked away and ignore her thoughts.

I have issues, and my issues have issues.

Before I can read more, the file is swiftly taken from my view. I look up to see the female FBI agent scowling. Annoyance rolls off her in waves.

"Sorry," I apologize and stick out my hand. "Makenna Goldwin."

Her thin lip curls at my outstretched hand as if it is covered with the worst possible diseases in medical history. The agent's brunette hair is tucked neatly into a bun, and aside from a bit of mascara, she wears no makeup. A professional. She's the true picture of professionalism. Perhaps I should take notes.

My eyebrows fly up as, yet again, I've run into another person who seems to not have been raised with manners.

That's it. This is the last time I wear these heels. Apparently, they aren't helping me build friendships in the professional world. Next time, I'm wearing pajamas and bunny slippers. Professionalism be damned.

"Agent Smith," she grumbles as if introducing herself to me is the last thing she expected would happen to her today. *Well, la-di-da to you, too, Agent Sassy Pants.*

Reaching over, she flips up the volume on a speaker box as Evo enters the tiny room. Following closely behind are two officers in uniform. They melt against the wall.

I don't pay much attention to the officers as my focus zooms in on the person sitting at the table. I had failed to notice there was a man in the hot seat when I entered the observation room.

This man is handsome, but there's something wild about him. Square jaw, sculpted lips, and tussled black hair, but his eyes . . .

He had been sitting as still as a statue, completely unaffected by being detained, and impervious to the fact that he is about to be questioned by a very large and intimidating FBI agent for crimes he may or may not have committed. In fact, he has a hint of a smug smile that sends chills up my arms and raises goose bumps on my skin.

Wild. Definitely wild. His body posture and attitude scream it. It isn't going to be hard reading this guy. The crazy ones are never hard to read, even when I just pass them by on the street.

I didn't exactly learn how to be a Micro-Expression specialist. For as long as I've known, I've had the ability to feel what others are feeling. Empathic? Perhaps, but it's not exactly what everyone thinks. People's feelings, truths, lies – it all just slithers over my skin like a snake. Once it reaches my skin I just *know.* That's the best way I can explain it. It is my curse, but I've used it to my advantage and built a meager career from it.

I've never told anyone about my extra ability. If I told anyone I have some kind of mutant freaky extra sense, one of two things would've happened. One: I would have been classified as insane. Two: I would end up being used. Hell, maybe both things would've happened. I wouldn't mind so much if I was committed to a nutter-house. They probably have free cookies. But I will never, in a million years, allow myself to be used and controlled by someone else.

With fluid grace for such a broad man, Evo sits in the plastic chair and leans back, casually observing the suspect's lack of behavior. The guy across from him is acting like they are about to have a cup of tea and talk about the weather. He is completely unmoved.

Cold blue eyes watch Evo with a calculating expression. Agent Smith spares me a small glance as I rub my arms when another chill hits my skin. Her annoyance toward me is annoying itself.

This guy radiates wrongness and it's not just because of his superior smugness or loathing of Evo. Something . . . else . . . is wrong with this guy. I can't put my finger on it.

"Chris Kenner," Evo begins, "I understand you have an active night life."

Kenner raises an eyebrow. "And?"

Recognizing the challenge in that one word, Evo stands to show who is in charge here, walks to the wall, and casually props himself against it with his arms folded. "The thing is, Mr. Kenner, everywhere you turn up, women disappear."

Kenner leans back in his chair. A tiny wave of *uncomfortable* slithers over my skin. He feels he's being discovered but is trying to hide it behind a relaxed posture. "And you think I have something to do with it?"

"As a matter of fact, yes. Yes, I do." Evo pushes off the wall and walks toward the table. Placing his hands on it, he towers over Kenner. I can see his muscles ripple under his long-sleeve shirt.

"I've had several witness accounts state that you were seen with each missing woman the night of their disappearance. No one knows who you are, and no one knows what you were doing or saying to their friend. But each of the witnesses saw you briefly chatting with their friend at the bar they were at and a few short hours later, their friend disappeared."

Kenner tilts forward, a challenge to Evo. "Just because someone saw me having a conversation with someone, doesn't mean I had anything to do with any missing women. I chat with many women, in a bar or otherwise. I'm a single, social guy." A small smug smile.

"Lie," I say quietly.

I feel his *deception* and it nearly seizes my breath. Agent Smith stares at me, but I pay her no attention because it seems that Evo and Agent Smith aren't the only ones who hear my announcement.

As I said the word, Chris Kenner's blue eyes had slowly lifted to the one-way window. As if he could have possibly heard me, he scans his eyes across its surface searching for the person who the voice belongs to.

Evo flips open a folder, giving no indication he heard me, nor that he's aware Kenner had heard me.

"Texas," Evo says, tossing clipped pictures of missing women in Kenner's direction. "Iowa, New York, Nevada, California, Illinois."

Kenner's smile grows. "These are not pictures of states, *Agent*." He says 'agent' mockingly, which leaves me confused. I look to Agent Smith, but her lips only twitch.

"These are pictures of faces," Kenner adds.

I can't see Evo's face, but I can feel his annoyance. It mingles with Kenner's wildness and lies. I imagine if I was in that room, I'd be twitchy with the smothering emotions.

"Don't try to be cute, Mr. Kenner." Evo jabs the table with his finger. "Each clip of pictures indicates the states from which those groups of missing women were taken. You were in each location. Each woman was last seen at a bar talking with you and then magically disappeared. You arrive, people disappear, and then you disappear. A few weeks later, you show up again, and the cycle repeats."

Kenner pushes the clipped pictures back to Evo. "I had nothing to do with their disappearances. I've never seen those women before."

"Both lies," I say after clearing my throat. He didn't even look at the pictures. It didn't take my freaky little extra sense to notice the lie.

"We know," Agent Smith whispers unnecessarily. She scratches her chin and sighs.

Kenner's eyes return to the one-way window before giving his attention back to Agent Johnson.

"Are you sure he can't see in here?" I ask Agent Smith.

In a bored tone, she replies, "No. It's a one-way glass."

I look to her, sweep my eyes from her head to her black glossy shoes. She appears relaxed. How is she unaffected by this guy? Doesn't he give her the creeps, too? Maybe she's just used to it. She does seem like the ball-busting type. I may be confident in my abilities of self-defense, but this is a chick I'm positive can hold her own.

"Then how do you explain this, Mr. Kenner? You have to understand how this looks for you."

Kenner inhales a deep breath and sighs loudly, as if he is bored with this interrogation. As if this is a waste of his time. I narrow my eyes.

Looking directly in Agent Johnson's eyes, he replies with a flat voice, "I've always wanted to travel, *Agent*." Again, he uses the mocking tone. "Touring this great country holds a great interest for me. The variations of different people and cultures are fascinating." He peers at the uniformed officers in the corner and I stiffen, waiting to see what he does.

"You're saying I'm abducting people, correct? I'm telling you I'm a traveler. Aside from the eye witness accounts that state I've been seen holding a conversation with these women, you have no evidence that I was the one who abducted them. You have no evidence that I have them, or took them anywhere. For all you know, they left by their own free will. What would I possibly do with a bunch of women surrounding me?"

"Oh, lord," I grunt quietly. Agent Smith hushes me.

He gives Evo a sadistic smile. "I'm sure you were also told that I was conversing with several people each night, not just women. In good faith, I even declined an attorney. Now, are we done here? You have no reason to keep me with your silly questions and accusations."

Blown away by the feeling of *truth*, I suck in a breath. Agent Smith looks at me pointedly. "All truth," I say aloud. "Though I feel like this was sneaky wording."

Evo stares at Kenner for a few moments, neither man backing down.

Begrudgingly, Evo says, "We're done." He briskly walks across the small room and slams the door on his exit. The walls quake from the force of it. Agent Smith and I walk out of the observation room to an angry Evo telling a man in uniform that Kenner is free to go.

"You're just releasing him?" I ask upon approach.

Evo turns to face us. He gestures us back into the observation room and leaves the door open once inside. His angry expression and emotion should be frightening but, oddly, I don't feel scared of him.

"He can't keep him," Agent Smith says.

"I have no choice." Evo scrubs his face tiredly. "The FBI has no evidence aside from witnesses saying they saw him talking to the missing women."

"Then why on earth did you call me here?" I throw my hands in the air.

Just as the words leave my mouth, Kenner walks by the observation room. The uniforms are leading him by the elbow. Our eyes catch each other's at the same time. He smirks a half smile. It is an arrogant evil smile that makes my stomach roll.

"I didn't call you here for his truths and lies to become evidence," Evo says, catching my attention again. "No offense, Ms. Goldwin, but your testimony wouldn't hold up in court. Human lie detectors can't be used as evidence. Especially when such a person has absolutely no real training in that line of work."

I growl, "Insulting me will get you nowhere, *Agent* Johnson."

His jaw tightens. "It's not my intention to insult you. I believe everything you told me tonight during the interrogation. I called you here because I wanted to confirm my own suspicions."

I return his glare. Even though I knew he spoke the truth, telling me how unimportant I am to the legal world still stings. "Right, well, since you're no longer in need of my services, I'll see myself out."

Pushing past him, I march out of the observation room and down the hall. My heels click on the white floor in a steady beat, but this time, the sound is satisfying. As I near the door, I hear another door shut behind me. Turning, I see Evo jog up to me. His sneakers leave rubber marks on the white tile.

I quirk an eyebrow as his scent whirls around me. It's woody, like he washes his clothes in pine.

Evo explains, "I'll be escorting you to the car. The world may not have evidence that Chris Kenner is abducting people, or worse, but you and I know better. The last thing we need is to have him see you unaccompanied."

"How gentleman-like of you," I snap.

In silence, we walk into the main lobby. Kenner has already disappeared, but I can still feel his lingering *wrongness*. Madam Mustache clutches her pens as she glares at me, and then nods to Evo with respect.

Evo holds the door open for me and I grunt my thanks as I walk through.

"Look, Ms. Goldwin," Evo begins, rubbing a hand through his short hair. The sky is dark now, stars twinkling above our heads. The city's smog has been whisked away with a nice breeze. The agent's slightly tousled short hair just adds to his attraction, and the breeze seemingly rakes its own fingers through it. I watch in fascination as his muscles ripple and his slightly raised shirt shows a very promising lower abdomen.

No! I chastise myself. *No ogling the FBI property*.

"Kenna," I correct him. Embarrassingly, my voice cracks. "Ms. Goldwin makes me sound like I am a fifty-year-old woman with nine cats, and Makenna is a mouthful."

He smiles as he tries out my nickname. "Kenna." He reaches for me and then thinks better of it. "Look, I didn't mean to jump down your throat in there. I'm under a lot of stress, and sometimes I unload that stress onto others."

Lips twitching, he seems like he wants to say more, possibly ask me a question, but he never does. I feel him fight with his emotions. Some are confusing to me as they caress my skin comfortingly.

I just stare at him. Stress is no excuse. I'm well versed in stressful situations, and I don't go around spreading my bad attitude. Okay, so sometimes I do, but he needs to muster up a mind to mouth filter.

Evo clears his throat when I don't acknowledge his apology. "Which car is yours?" he asks.

Without waiting for him, I begin walking again, heading toward my hunk of junk. It isn't the most professional car, but it sure beats not having one at all. It took me months to save up for another car when my last one took a dump in the middle of the ghetto. That's an experience I never want to repeat.

As I put my key in the car and unlock it, I see in the merger reflection of the window that he's rocking back and forth on his heels, clearly on the verge of saying what he has been battling himself about.

I turn to him, my hair whipping me in my face. "Spit it out, Agent Johnson."

He smiles at my blunt attitude. "Are you hungry?" he asks, rocking back on his heels and holding the pose. He's nervous about how I will take his question.

I gape like a fish. Is this guy trying to ask me out? Sure, he may be gorgeous, but the dude just insulted what I do for a living.

I step closer to him which clearly is a mistake. He smells amazing. Out in the open like we are, the pine scent is far more noticeable, and it tickles my insides in a tingly sort of way. There are other scents too, but I can't pinpoint what the smell is. It's pure masculinity though, and a whole lot of pheromones.

"I don't know who taught you how to pick up women, Agent Romeo, but let me give you some advice. You don't ask a girl out within minutes of insulting her."

"Call me Evo."

I roll my eyes. "Look, I'm exhausted and these heels are killing me." I open my car door and dig in the center compartment. My fingers grasp a cold pencil and a receipt for bread and cheese. I lay it flat against my car window and scribble across it as fast as I can.

"This is my number." I thrust the receipt at him. "If you need my services again, you can reach me here."

"Mm-hmm." His gaze flicks over the barely readable phone number.

"So if that's all –" I grab my door and it squeaks as I open it wider.

"And if I want to try asking you out again?" he asks with a wicked-hot grin that licks my insides. I can feel his arousal for me beat against my own skin, adding to my already liquidity. I look around us, as if at any moment, someone will come and save me from this conversation. And this man.

I need to get away from him before we both do something we will regret by morning.

When I look back to him, he's leaning toward me. I swear he takes a sniff. I freeze, trying to remember if I put on deodorant this morning.

"What the hell is wrong with you?" I snarl.

His grin grows wider as he retreats into his own space. "I *will* keep asking you out, Kenna. Eventually, you will say yes. I always get my way. You're a conundrum to me and I enjoy a good puzzle."

I gulp. "Right. Well. I'm ah . . . I'm gonna go now. It was nice meeting you, Evo."

Effectively dismissing him, I hop in the car, shut the door, and manually roll down my windows. The heat from the day's temperature made my car stifling despite the evening's cooler breeze.

Roaring the engine to life, I nod my goodbye awkwardly, leave the parking space, and glance at my rearview mirror while I drive away. Evo is walking back into the police station, a smug smile on his face. I blow out a deep breath, not realizing I had been holding it.

CHAPTER TWO

Makenna Goldwin

Entering my little apartment, I kick my door shut and quickly survey my dark surroundings. I had locked the door when I went to the police station, but stranger things have happened to me. I'm a lightning rod for bad luck and it wouldn't be the first time I interrupted a robber in the midst of robbing.

After the interrogation this evening, I'm still feeling a little edgy. These sorts of things don't usually affect me. Those sorts of people, either. I've met my fair share of nasty folk and I've always had the ability to remain calm during a crisis. But there was something about Chris Kenner that had left me and my alter ego on edge. A lingering effect, like a bad aftertaste. The drive home and the breeze freely whipping my hair did nothing to whisk it away.

My apartment is neat and tidy. The only thing I don't accept from myself is disorganization. I like having everything just so, and I don't like to leave things unfinished. It makes me feel more put together than I know I am.

My furniture is centered around my T.V. and all my papers are stacked in neat piles. There's not a single dirty dish in the sink or leftover food laying on the counter.

My apartment contains the bare essentials – a sofa, TV, a small dining room table, and a bed. I can't afford anything else and honestly, I don't need more than I have. My only complaint is that I can hear everything that's happening in the apartment above mine, and beside mine. Babies crying. Couples arguing. Beds slamming repeatedly against the wall. There's never a feeling of true privacy, but that's what I get with such a pathetic wage.

I slip off my heels and pad to my trash can, dumping them inside with a loud thump. Never again will I talk myself into looking professional for other people's benefit. If they don't think I can be a private investigator in more practical clothing, then they aren't someone I want to work with. It's not like business is booming. Most of my clients are just your average Joe and Jane.

Sometimes . . . sometimes, I dream about giving it all up. If I had the means to, I think I would.

I don't even know how Evo came across my information. Being a referral only, my client list is small and I consider my office to be the couch in front of my TV. I guess it doesn't really matter.

Fifteen minutes later, and I'm still thinking about Evo. My anxiety is beginning to make me fidgety and I drum my fingers on the counter as I wait for the microwave to finish cooking my frozen meal.

Evo, Evo, Evo. I don't have a clue who he is aside from being an FBI agent. I didn't see a wedding ring on his finger, so I know he doesn't have a woman at home. The last thing I need is to be labeled a homewrecker. Not that I want to have sex with him. Oh no – I never once thought about licking his skin to see if he tasted as good as he smelled. Or running my hands over his body to see if his muscles were as hard as they looked. Or unzipping his pants with my teeth to see if his bulge . . .

No! I scold myself, giving my head a shake to clear the erotic images. My alter ego feels smug about my train of thought and I thump my hand against the counter. It seems she has a thing for the blond hunk. I'm doing my best to ignore her urges, but it's proving difficult when my own thoughts are stuck on him.

I sit down on my couch with my meal and exhale with relief. The bed in the apartment above mine begins to rock. I glare up at the ceiling as paint chips break away and pepper my carpet like falling snow. I roll my shoulders and try to block it about by thinking of this evening's main event.

Kenner is something to worry about. Sadism was oozing from his pores. I'm certain he had taken those women. What I'm not certain of is what he was doing with them. A man with obvious sociopathic tendencies doesn't just abduct women for fun, and he definitely fits the sociopath label.

His handsome face and wicked grin surfaces in my mind, and I grip my fork a bit too tight.

My muscles tense and I attempt to breathe through it. I just have to hope it will blow over. This is no longer my case. I was called in as a human lie detector, and that's it. He doesn't know my name.

But he saw your face, a little voice inside my head tells me. *He saw your face. He heard your voice. That's all he needs.*

The fork pauses halfway to my open mouth. Imaginings of what he may have done to those women makes my insides roll. Then, imaginings of him taking *me.*

My anxiety kicks into high gear. It pumps through my veins in waves of heated adrenaline. The fork falls from my hand as my fingers shake and my heart thumb-thumps painfully in my chest. I know what this means. I know what this is. And I'm powerless to stop it.

The doctors call it anxiety attacks. They're wrong. Deep down I know it's much more than that. Not only does my stomach feel like it's being raked from the inside out, but *she* tends to start having extreme emotions and meltdowns that don't quite fit the situation. Any situation.

When I feel threatened, *she* can react like this. My alter ego's thoughts drown out my own. I can't function normally like this – not with her. I can't even find someone attractive without her emotional input. It's like having two of me inside my head – my alter ego and me – but I have no control over the thoughts and feelings that aren't my own. If her emotions are extreme enough, if I'm threatened enough, the pain begins, and it takes everything I have, plus prescribed medication, to subdue them.

If I give in to this panic attack, or whatever this is, the other side of me is completely sure she can keep me safe. *Us* safe. *Us* . . .

I cry out and clench my stomach. I can feel her pacing inside me, restlessly snarling. I try to reassure her with rational thoughts, with bunnies and rainbows because that's the only thing I can think of in such pain. I might as well be talking to a brick wall or rabid animal.

My situation sounds insane, even to me. I fight it. I clench my teeth and fight it. A groan escapes my resolve and I double over. Food flies off my plate as it hits the ground. The plate cracks with an audible clank, and I've vaguely aware of the gravy spreading across the carpet.

Feeling like my insides are being ripped to shreds with a million tiny knives, I reach for my pills on the edge of the coffee table. My vision blurs. My hands shake. I almost knock the yellow bottle over.

Once in my grasp, I tip a double dose of prescribed anxiety medicine into my palm and swallow them without water. It doesn't take long before it kicks in and I'm out like a light. As the blackness invades like a rush of water, I just know that tomorrow a migraine will be my ever-present companion.

Evo Johnson

Shutting my car door, I'm greeted by a familiar scent. I turn around and see Ben leaning against my car, his arms folded across his chest. As always, he's as silent as they come. By now, I know better than to be startled by his sudden appearance. His short black hair blows in the slight breeze that carries the sweet aroma of pine, dirt, and the nearby creek.

I note he's only in a pair of shorts and the moon glints across his chest. "Perimeter run?"

Benjamin Grobin is my beta of the Cloven Pack. He and I are always the last ones in before the night watch comes on duty. When I'm away, part of his job is acting as alpha for the pack. He takes his job very seriously, never leaving an ounce of time for anything normal people would consider fun. Women, parties, beer. Their appeal rolls right off him. I consider him to be a workaholic and often tease him about it, because whenever I return, he gives me a full report. Rattles it right off like a marine.

Ben never missing a beat, not for as long as I've known him.

"Dyson just took over perimeter before you pulled in. How'd it go? Were you able to get ahold of the witch?"

That's the funny thing about packs – we never keep anything from each other. There's no point. What one member does from day to day affects the whole pack because we operate as one unit. Every wolf knows when someone leaves the property, where they're going, and with whom they are meeting. They've probably spent the entire evening discussing what I was doing while I was gone.

My eyebrows pull together in irritation.

"What?" Ben asks.

"I don't think Makenna Goldwin is a witch."

Ben huffs and shifts his weight. The gravel of the driveway shifts under his bare feet. "And why do you think that? Is she not an empath?" He bases his opinions on facts instead of speculation. It's this trait that makes him a great beta, but not such a great people-person.

I lean against the car with him, scanning the trees out of habit. "She had no idea I was a wolf shifter. She would have known and confronted me about it when we first met. You know how the witches and shifters don't talk with one another, let alone be in the same room together." His nose twitches and I press on. "There's something more about her and I just can't put my finger on it. She smells different." Not to mention my wolf stands at attention when she's near like some whipped puppy. I'm not going to tell Ben that, though. The last thing I need is to have him go digging for more information about her before I have the chance to myself.

Her scent was intoxicating. No way am I going to mention that to Ben, either. I'd never hear the end of it, lusting after a human. Gifted or not, we don't mix species. The witches may mix their blood, but the wolves can't. Our community survives on secrecy, and dating a human threatens that. We wouldn't be able to have pups with them if we tried. I consider situations like that entirely irresponsible.

We stand in silence for a little while, breathing in the cool air. Crickets chirp to one another, irritating songs that grate against my every nerve.

"What do you think she is?" Ben finally asks. "And what did the FBI need help with this time?"

Ignoring his first question because I'm still working it out myself, I give him a brief rundown. Confidential information is never wise to keep from your pack, especially if it involves wolf shifters. That, and Ben will hound me until I give him details.

In what feels like a past life, I had been an FBI agent. After a brief call from my sister, I discovered what my father was doing to the pack, came home, and challenged him for the alpha position. The challenge resulted in his death, a matter I will never regret. I shouldn't have left in the first place. I knew what kind of man he was. He deserves more than death, and I hope that if an afterlife exists, justice found him.

He had been a cruel leader and was financially, physically, and emotionally running the pack into the ground. With my new responsibility, my career in the FBI had effectively ended. I don't miss it, but from time to time, I help the agency if there isn't an interrogator in the area.

"They think some guy is abducting people all over the country."

Ben looks at me. "I see. And is he?"

"Yes, but there's no real proof." I rub my hands over my face. "That's not all. He's a rogue."

Ben sucks in a breath. "Shit."

Rogues are wolf shifters who have no pack. Whether they choose that life on their own or have no choice but to leave their pack, most of the time they turn into a beast, both man and wolf. Some can cope without the support of other shifters – some even prefer it – but most become maniacs.

"What information do you have?" Ben asks, straightening his posture. In a split second, he switched from my friend to duties.

"He's abducting women, Ben. For the life of me, I can't figure out why or what he's doing with them. Completely innocent people, randomly selected, all attending bars. The last known bar was Be Deviled."

"The Riva Pack's bar?"

I nod. "Their friends see him talking to the victim and then poof, they disappear before the night is over. He was completely deranged. Any wolf who sat at a police station for crimes that could expose the race should be sweating. Instead, he found his situation humorous and tried provoking me." I look at him. "Do me a favor. Check out this Chris Kenner. See what pack he was originally from and what you can figure out as to why he no longer belongs to one."

Ben heads for the house at a jog. House is putting it mildly. It's a mansion on the outside but holds several living quarters on the inside. The mansion exterior is meant to look like one giant home for human eyes.

The white siding seemingly shimmers in the daylight, but at night, it's shadowed and mysterious under a black shingled roof. A large shaded front porch with pillars is our safe haven on nice days, the porch swing my sister's favorite destination. Surrounding the home is our territory, acres of wooded area riddled with creeks and wildlife. We replaced the landscape last year with new rock and vegetation, making the home more inviting. In truth, I wanted to wash away as much of what my father had done as I could. Too many memories happened in these lawns. Memories I'd rather forget. Beatings I can still feel on my backside.

My eyes roam over the windows, some light, some dark. My father's memory is almost gone. Almost. And Kelsey, one of our wolves, does very well with the upkeep and making this place feel like it should: A home.

The Cloven Pack has only one mated couple and five other unmated wolves, besides me. When I took the alpha position, a few mated pairs felt free enough to leave and begin a new life in a different pack. There were no hard feelings whatsoever and I wished them well with their new packs.

Taking a deep breath, I try to let go of some of the tension left in my shoulders. Kenner is enough of a distraction, but the only thing my mind and wolf can seem to focus on is Makenna.

She baffles me. Her scent is off for a human, but I am sure she isn't a witch. Witches always know when they're in the presence of a shifter and are always bold enough to say so. Not that Makenna wasn't bold. She has a wicked tongue, but I know she has no idea I'm a wolf.

She's sexy as hell, too. I could tell she was uncomfortable in her professional attire, pulling and itching at the hem of her skirt. It made me wonder what she preferred to wear. Her long brown hair is wavy and her deep brown eyes are inviting, totally opposite to her prickly attitude. She isn't tiny, but I can tell she is toned with curves in all the right places.

So, if she's not a witch and doesn't smell totally human, what is she? And why can't I get her off my mind?

I wake to my phone ringing.

Peaking open one eye, I glance at the clock on the cable box below the TV. It's past noon. I slept on the couch the entire night and morning. That usually happens when I'm forced to take my pills. Still, I scowl. This seems to be a lot lately and my body is beginning to feel the effects of the lumpy couch. It's not the most comfortable place to sleep.

Groaning, I roll over and grab my phone off the floor. "-Llo?" I manage to croak out.

"Makenna Goldwin? Private investigator?" a woman asks.

"Yeah." I sit up, forcing my voice to be clearer. My foot lands in half dried gravy and I suppress a gag.

"My name is Johanna Clark. I would like to hire you." *Straight to business. My kind of woman.*

"One moment." I gingerly stretch and let my body slither off the couch. Entering the kitchen, I switch on the coffee machine. I'm definitely going to need my beloved dark caffeine if I plan to be functional today.

"What can I help you with, Ms. Clark?" I reach into the cupboard and grab my one and only mug. As I wait for her to respond, I kiss the ceramic mug and impatiently curl my toes against the curling kitchen tile.

"Oh, please, call me Johanna, dear." Lips still pressed to ceramic, I freeze, internally bucking at the endearment. I'm not so fond of pet names, kind-hearted or not.

"My granddaughter is missing. She went out with a few friends last night and never came home. The police tell me it's too soon to raise any alarm. My Cassie is an adult and could just be staying at a friend's house. They aren't ready to start investigating yet. I checked with some of her friends. They haven't seen her since last night," Johanna pauses for a moment, seemingly taking a breath. Perhaps I should have grabbed a notepad. I eye the pen and paper on my dining table and nibble at my lip, torn between the caffeine and my duties.

"The police might be –"

"I know my Cassie, Ms. Goldwin. She has a rambunctious streak, but she's never been irresponsible. She would have called if she planned to not come home. I'm all she has left, you see. She wouldn't leave me worried like this. Not on purpose." Johanna sniffles into the phone.

"Don't you worry Ms. – er – Johanna. I'll do my best to find your granddaughter. It might be best if you and I could meet so I can get more details."

"Of course, dear. Would the city park in an hour be okay?"

I check the clock on the oven. That should be enough time to shower and drive the twenty minutes over there. "That should work fine. I'll be waiting for you on the bench just before the trail. It's the bench that overlooks the water."

"Yes, I know the one. My late husband and I would go there often back in our day." She giggles. "I'll see you there, dear."

She hangs up before I can correct her and supply my first name. I pull the phone away and frown at it before setting it down on the counter. Filling my mug with fresh coffee, I sit at the table and flip open my laptop, firing it up. I search the police station's website for missing people in our area, and, sure enough, no one named Cassie is on it. Not a big surprise. It was a long shot if I've ever tried one.

There are, however, a few very recent reports of missing people. The most recent listings are all women. I wonder if these women are a part of the clipped photographs Evo had presented to Chris last night.

Police have protocols to follow. Cassie's disappearance hasn't met those requirements, so they wouldn't have it on their website yet. They can't report it and begin a search until then. I understand that. Some people who are reported missing by loved ones aren't actually missing and will show up within a day or so. Usually drunk. Or high. Or both.

I shrug, jostling the table and the coffee inside my cup.

Finding Cassie's social media account was easy enough. Tagged fresh pictures are loaded from last night's bar adventure and I sip from my dark delicious brew as I study each photo, trying to commit faces to memory.

Next, I do a web search of Johanna Clark. It's always best to know who you're working for. Other than her name mentioned on her deceased husband's online obituary, there's not much else to go on besides a current address.

Storing her phone number in my phone directory, I add her address with it.

I down the rest of my coffee and I head for the shower in a hurry. A half hour later, I sit on a bench overlooking the water. It's a beautiful but humid afternoon, and the bugs are persistent as they buzz around my ears. No matter how many times I swat at them, they still come back.

The water laps at a dock that's seen better days and I watch as tiny bubbles foam around the dock's wood edge. No one else is around, which isn't surprising given it is a weekday and most people are still at work, so I drink in the peace. The calm. The song of the birds and the heat of the sun.

Not five minutes after I get lost in my own thoughts, I hear footsteps approach behind me. I glance back and stand once I realize it's an elderly lady making her way in my direction. She has to be in her early seventies, give or take. She's in good shape and doesn't need any assistance walking, though I detect a hint of a shuffle. Wrinkles line her skin and short salon-styled white curls frame her head.

"Johanna Clark?" I hold out my hand once she's a few feet in front of me.

She gives me a warm smile and shakes my hand. Taking a seat on the bench, she gestures for me to do the same. "It's nice to meet you, Ms. Goldwin."

I take the chance to correct her, hoping to stave off any more future endearments. "Please, call me Kenna." I return her warm smile, but on my own face, it feels like a grimace.

"Wonderful. Such a beautiful name for such a beautiful young lady, dear." I mentally sag as my efforts prove fruitless.

She pulls out a picture from her pocket. "This is my Cassie, taken last year." She holds the picture out for me to take. The young woman staring back at me is just an average girl. Mousy brown hair with plain features. I recognize her from her social media page.

"She's very pretty, Johanna. You must be proud." As tears line her eyes, I'm pummeled with her waves of sorrow. I press on quickly. "What can you tell me about Cassie?"

Johanna lets out a sigh and turns her head to look at the water before us. "I've been Cassie's guardian since my daughter passed away. Cassie was only ten years old. Cancer, you know." She looks at me pointedly, like I should have guessed it myself. I nod.

"Cassie has always been such a well-behaved girl. Her father has never met her, and frankly, I don't even know who he is."

"I see," I say, urging her to continue as she seems to be lost in her memories.

"Cassie just finished college this year. Her friends decided to throw a get together at one of the bars last night to celebrate before everyone went off to work in the real world. Be Deviled, I believe it was called." She giggles. "Who would call a bar Be Deviled. Sounds like a deviled egg recipe."

I grin. I can't help it.

"Of course, Cassie attended. She is always such a loyal person and wouldn't miss saying goodbye to the friends she made before everyone went their separate ways."

"Do you happen to know if that's the only bar they went to?"

"Her friends say so. It seems to be a popular bar among college students. Humor has it its under new management and they plan to change their entry polices. I gather it's more popular for the name than anything else."

"Oh yes, I've heard of it." I have. And frankly, I'm surprised they were brave enough to go there. It's not geared toward Cassie's sort of crowd. I'm even more surprised they stayed as long as they did. "Do you have any names or contact numbers of the friends who were there with her?"

Johanna digs in her pocket again and produces a folded note. "I wrote down the ones I know personally. I couldn't tell you each and every one of her friends' names or their cellular numbers, but I figured this would get you somewhere." She hands the crinkled list over. "This just isn't like my Cassie. She has always been responsible and never has been in any trouble. I know my Cassie, Kenna. She would have never left me worrying about her. She would have called by now. I fear something terrible has happened to her."

Her grief slithers over my skin. She truly believes Cassie is in terrible danger.

Missing women. Missing women turning up everywhere.

I'm beginning to think last night and today's events aren't by accident. How could I think otherwise? Women are disappearing; I just so happened to aid in the interview of psycho boy last night and then Johanna calls me this morning – it's too coincidental.

If Johanna is right and Cassie is a responsible girl, then something could have happened to her. I'd bet my last dollar Chris Kenner is involved here. I suppose there's one way I could find out quickly . . .

I briefly think about finding some way to contact Evo, but then quickly dismiss the idea. Johanna contacted me, not them. If the police aren't going to contact or involve Evo's team, then neither will I. The last thing I need is to have that guy involved in my investigation. I find him too much of a distraction.

I curl the note into my palm. Nope, it wouldn't do to have him involved.

My alter ego thinks otherwise, though. she's intrigued by my returning thoughts of Evo and urges me to seek him out. I quickly shove my thoughts, and hers, aside before it becomes all consuming. There's a very good chance I'll never see him again. She needs to come to terms with that.

I pat Johanna's shoulder. Sympathy has never been my strong suit, even if it's well deserved. "I'll do my best to find out for you, Johanna. I can't guarantee anything but try to stay positive."

CHAPTER THREE

Makenna Goldwin

That evening I wait in a family diner just before closing time. I had researched her friends, asked around, and got a job location of the first friend on the list.

Jackie is Cassie's long-time best friend. She's a waitress for this twenty-four-hour diner. Having returned to my apartment to search on social media, I found a profile picture of Jackie and headed over to the diner during her shift. I need to ask questions, but I want to wait until the crowd dies down, so she'll have time to answer them without neglecting her tables.

And wouldn't you know it, my waitress happens to be Jackie. Fate has a funny way of working out sometimes. It won't be as hard as I thought it might be to pull her away for a few minutes.

Sipping my coffee, I take in the activity around me. The tables are starting to become bare, but the kitchen sounds as busy as ever. Plates, cups, and silverware clink together. I do my best to ignore it, but without much chatter happening and bodies to muffle the sound, its loud.

The restaurant hasn't been updated in years. The white tables are yellowing and the bright red booth cushions are cracked. The staff are able to wear their regular clothing, too. It's tacky and shows that whoever owns the diner has a lack of interest in professionalism. I frown as my own hypocrisy dawns on me. Didn't I just toss my heels in the trash and threaten to wear bunny slippers to work?

To the people eating their meals, I probably look like a loner sitting here drinking my coffee while I watch those around me. I witness a mom kiss her tired son's boo-boo, a husband and wife quietly having an intimate conversation, and the waiters gossiping. Each person I feel a sense of longing for. Not for them, of course, but for what they have: a family, a loved one, friends. Those are things I lack in my life, current and past. They are everything I secretly want for myself, yet don't dare dream of. I've never had the privilege of these things and the thought makes my heart ache.

I can feel all their emotions, too. It used to be too much for me when I was younger and would often overwhelm my thoughts and sense of peace. But after a while, I learned to separate their emotions from making changes in my own.

My phone beeps, breaking me out of my survey of those around me. I pull it out of my pocket and swipe the screen to find I have a message from an unsaved number.

You look like you could use some company.

A little miffed, I glance around me at the tables. When I notice that no one is paying me any attention, my eyes drift toward the door.

Propped against the wall is Evo. I draw in a breath. That guy would look sexy even if he was sporting a slasher costume. How did he find me and how long has he been watching me?

Giving me a sexy lopsided grin, he walks over to my table and takes the seat opposite of mine. My cheeks heat. He's dressed in sweatpants and a sweatshirt, an attire completely identical to my own. Once seated, his pine scent washes over me, and seemingly against my will, butterflies flutter in my stomach.

"I don't remember inviting you," I grit through my teeth. "I'm working. You need to leave." Even though every part of my being wants him to stay.

He continues to smile at me. "What kind of gentlemen would I be if I left a lady to dine on her own?"

I glare at him. "I'm not exactly dining. How did you find me?"

He leans back in his seat, completely unaffected by my hostile attitude. "All the right friends in all the right places."

Cocky bastard.

"Right. Well, why don't you call up one of those friends and go bug them instead." I give him a tiny wave, letting him know he's been dismissed.

I need to lose this guy if I plan to get any answers from Jackie. People are always reluctant to talk to strangers and the fewer strangers who are asking the questions, the more open they'll be to discuss their nightlife. Even if one of the strangers is panty dropper.

Just one look at him and any girl knows a night in bed with this stranger will promise things they'd never experienced. Delicious things. Forbidden things. I shudder. Things I never thought I needed or wanted.

His grin widens, and to my horror, I know it's because I'm staring.

"Is there anything I can get you, sir?" I tear my gaze from my erotically distracting, albeit unwanted, companion as freckle-faced Jackie closes the distance to our table.

Keeping his eyes on me, he replies, "I'll also have a coffee."

I watch her leave, my shoulders sagging. I had planned to talk to her when she came back for a refill.

He catches onto my frustration easily. "Does our waitress hold some sort of fascination to you?"

"I told you – I'm working. I need to talk to her and you being here is messing that up."

He leans forward, putting his elbows on the table after Jackie places his hot mug in front of him. "Is it that I'll mess up your interview or is it that you find me . . . distracting?"

I roll my eyes, fully intending to not answer his question. I'm like a glass wall. A damn glass wall and he can see right through me.

He chuckles. "So, what's the job?" His tone is seductive, and it pulls me in.

"Sorry, but I don't reveal my investigations to FBI," I say quietly – embarrassingly meekly. Has his eyes always been so . . . warm? I straighten and clear my throat. "If my clients wanted to involve the FBI, they'd call you. It'd be unprofessional of me to bring in a government agency to assist in *my* investigation." *Not to mention I'm a territorial bitch who never understood the concept of sharing.*

Evo leans back again, narrowing his eyes. "I'm surprised you haven't researched me. I'm not with the FBI – not anymore. I haven't been for a while, actually."

Was I blind last night? "Excuse me?"

"I'm a retired agent. I only give a hand when they call and ask."

A retired agent? He doesn't look more than a few years older than me. Can someone retire from the FBI at such an early age? I match his narrowed gaze. What does someone have to do to 'retire' from the FBI so young?

"You like to play cops and robbers? You must enjoy living a fantasy life. Good to know." I can't help but verbally poke him. Age aside, if someone retires from something, that generally means they no longer work there. I take a sip from my coffee, feeling triumphant and important.

"Yep." He pops his lips, totally unfazed. "So, that means I'm free to help you out."

"Um, no," I quickly quip. I'm taken back by his suggestion. An active agent isn't someone I want to partner with, but a retired one will be hard to refuse. Especially if he's able to get more information than I can. *Damn it all to hell.*

"Common, Kenna," he says, returning to that seductive tone once more. "Tell me what's going on."

I sigh loudly, the breath ruffling a stray hair. It wouldn't be smart of me to refuse his help, pain in the ass or not. "A girl went missing last night." He raises his eyebrows in surprise. "I'm here to question Jackie, who's her best friend, about what she witnessed or if she witnessed anything at all." I slide Cassie's picture to him. "Her name is Cassie Clark. She was last seen last night with her friends at a bar called Be Deviled."

Recognizing the name, he stiffens, then recovers just as quickly.

"You know the place?"

"Yes," he says after a moment. "They shouldn't have been there."

I double blink.

"Do you think Chris Kenner has anything to do with it?" he asks.

I squint my eyes at him with suspicion. I don't need him running back to his FBI buddies to tell them there's possibly another missing woman. I promised Johanna I would keep this private unless she wanted to expand her search by returning to law enforcement resources.

He holds up his hands. "No need to get so touchy. I don't plan to involve the FBI unless you find it necessary. I understand that you'd be protective of your clients."

Satisfied at his truth, I give a curt nod. "I have my suspicions that this could be Chris Kenner related, but I have yet to interview any of her friends."

I am almost one hundred percent positive it was Chris, but I'm not going to tell him that. Not only do I know nothing about Evo, but I don't fully trust him yet. Just because he's telling the truth about not running off to his buddies and spilling the beans, doesn't mean he won't decide to do it later. People go back on their word all the time. I would know. I had it happen to me plenty of times as a kid.

Jackie comes over to refill my coffee and glances down at the picture on the table. She sucks in a sharp breath. "You know Cassie Clark?" she asks Evo who still has the picture in front of him.

He shifts his eyes to me, a silent gesture that she's directing her questions to the wrong person.

I clear my throat to gain her attention. "Yes, that's actually why I'm – we're – here. Johanna Clark, Cassie's grandmother, asked me to look into Cassie's whereabouts. I came here to ask you a few questions."

Jackie glances around the diner. She pulls over a chair from a nearby table and runs a hand through her hair. "Yes, Cassie and I know each other, known each other since we were little kids. She's my best friend. I don't understand where she could be, though. It's not like her to just disappear. She hasn't been answering any of my calls."

This is easier than I thought it'd be. Jackie seems to be opening right up. I can feel her genuine worry for her missing friend. She has no idea what happened to Cassie. This means I can cross her off as a possible suspect. It's unbelievable how many times friends verbally fight and the next day one of them has a literal knife sticking out of their back. Maybe not that exact scenario, but close enough.

"When did you last see her?"

"Last night, we were all at Be Deviled." She pauses, eyes glued to Cassie's picture. "We all went there as a going away party or whatever. Just before I was going to leave, I turned around to ask Cassie if she needed a ride and she wasn't there. I thought she just went home and I didn't hear her tell me goodbye. That place can get pretty loud. Full of . . . different people. But when Johanna called me this morning, I started to freak out."

Evo chimes in and shifts toward Jackie. Quietly, he asks, "Did you see her talking to anyone you didn't know?"

Jackie's eyes tilt up as she searches her memories across the water-stained ceiling. "She talked to a lot of people last night. Cassie is nowhere near ready to settle down and find a guy, but that doesn't hold her back from flirting with them." At my raised eyebrows, she corrects herself. "Oh, don't get me wrong, she's not . . . slutty or anything. She hardly ever sleeps with a guy. But like every single girl, she enjoys the chase. And attention."

"Er – right." I run my tongue across my teeth. "Okay, so did any one of these guys stand out? Did she ever go outside with one of them? Did she ever show a particular interest in any?"

She thinks again, rubbing her bottom lip with her index finger. "There was this one guy who pulled her on the dance floor. He was, like, extremely hot. I didn't think much of it at the time, but he spent a good amount of time whispering in her ear as they danced. After that, he bought her a drink and then left. I remember her saying how confusing that was because they seemed to hit it off and then he just went home."

Evo nods. "What did this guy look like?"

Jackie taps her chin. "Tall, dark, and handsome. I remember he had the lightest blue eyes. Even though he was hot, he sort of gave me the creeps. Cassie didn't care, though. She can be attracted to the occasional bad boy."

That sounds like Kenner to me. Evo and I spare each other a knowing glance. "This is all very helpful, Jackie. My name is Kenna. If you remember any more details or if Cassie returns your call –" I pause, looking for a pen and paper.

Evo pulls my receipt from his pocket and says, "please don't hesitate to call her. Anything you think of could be helpful."

I glare at him.

She nods and stands up. "My shift is almost over. I should probably finish my work. Look, I appreciate you trying to find her. I have this terrible feeling that something bad has happened to her. If you need me for anything, you can find me here most nights. Please, try to find her." She turns and heads back to the diner's kitchen.

"Was that the receipt I gave you?" I hiss at him. "The one with my number on it?"

A grin slowly spreads across his face. "Your number is in my phone now."

"Should I be worried?"

He laughs and the sound twists my insides into a knotted mess. I slump in my seat and quickly change the subject. "Tall, dark, handsome, and creepy sounds extremely familiar, don't ya think?"

"M-hmm."

"What?" I ask him when his continued staring starts to make me feel uncomfortable.

He cocks his head to the side. "Are you dating anybody?"

"Come – Come again?" I splutter.

He shrugs nonchalantly. "Just trying to get to know you better. Since we will be working together and all."

"You do know that I can tell when someone isn't being completely honest, right?"

"How does that work, exactly?" He invades my space like a curious toddler, pressing his stomach into the table as he scoots closer. "Is it genetic? Can you turn it off and on?"

I blow out a breath. "It's a constant part of me. There is no off and on switch. I feel what everyone is feeling all the time, whether I want to or not. I wouldn't know if it's genetic – I don't know anything about my birth parents, let alone my heritage. All I know is it's an extra little sense that isn't as convenient as it sounds."

"I imagine it must be difficult to always know what someone else is feeling," he says, dazzling me with a wicked smile. "What am I feeling right now?"

I don't want to answer his question. I don't want to tell him that his *lust* for me is licking its way up my arms and clogging my coherent thinking. Giving him the satisfaction of letting him know that I know he wants me, isn't a can of worms I want to open right now, even if my alter ego – and my treacherous body – want him, too. So instead, I stare at him blankly, letting him know I'm not going to play his game. And games are definitely something this hunk likes to play.

He frowns when he understands the meaning behind my silence. "You don't let a lot of people in, do you, baby." It is said as a statement instead of a question.

"Baby?" I ask, my eyebrows flying up.

"Must be a lonely life you've got going," he continues, ignoring my surprise at the new nickname.

"I wouldn't know any other way. I've been alone my whole life, even when I was surrounded by people."

His jaw ticks at my confession. I can feel his lust replaced with anger on my behalf. He doesn't like that I was alone. It's not like it's something I could help. At least not when I was a kid. Now, my loner lifestyle is out of necessity so I won't have to worry about further disappointment and heartache.

After Evo pays for our coffee, he again walks me to my car. It must have rained while I was inside because small puddles are pocketed between cracks in the concrete. Our sneakers splash against them with each stride.

"You should really get a more reliable car."

I frown, stopping in my tracks. "What's wrong with my car?"

"Are you serious?" He points. "That thing looks like a small gust of wind would tear it apart."

"Hunk has always been faithful and reliable. She'll get me from point A to point B and that's all I need."

He laughs. "Hunk is an appropriate name for this scrap of metal, but it's definitely not a reliable car. You should consider retiring this . . . thing to the junk yard and buy something more . . . suitable."

Heat flares in my cheeks. "Not everyone can afford the luxury of just going out and purchasing a new car simply because the car they have is covered in rust."

He holds up his hands to my spitting words. "I suppose you're right." Then abruptly adds, "I'll just have to buy you a new one."

My mouth falls open. I know it does because the damp air licks at my tongue.

I poke him in his very large chest and invade his space. When his scent reaches my nostrils and my finger hits his pure steel muscles, I almost forget what I was going to say. His body is as hard as it looks.

"Buddy, I don't even know you. I'm starting to think your mother completely forgot to teach you manners. You don't march around offering to buy cars for strangers. Especially when that stranger just told you they couldn't afford to buy a new car. It makes them feel low. I don't need that shit in my life, and I sure as hell don't need anyone to take care of me. This stranger can take care of herself."

I feel his lust slither across my skin as I poke him one last time. Amusement lights his features. "You've got a mean streak, you know that?" Affectionately tucking a stray hair behind my ear, he adds, "As for not knowing you, I'd like to rectify that. Have breakfast with me. Tomorrow morning." It isn't so much a question as it is a demand. In fact, I feel the demand ripple along my skin, making my own lust reach for the surface. Freaking odd treacherous, treacherous body. And his fingers, calloused from hard work, caress the side of my cheek as he trails them from my ear to my jaw.

"Absolutely not," I say unconvincingly.

Confused, he cocks his head to the side and inhales. That's twice now he's sniffed me, and I vow to check my soap when I get home. Before I can think further on that, he shakes his head and replies, "Pick you up at eight."

He swiftly walks away, not giving me any choice in the matter. It only leaves me thoroughly ticked off and confused at his odd behavior.

Sensuous lust now vacated, I stomp two steps to my car, pull the door open, and get in. I drive across the cracks in the pavement and the car jostles me about, but I barely notice it. On the drive home, I spit and fume, trying desperately to think of anything else besides Evo. Even as I lay wide awake in my own bed, listening to my neighbor's newborn wail for another bottle, the touch of his fingers still lingers on my jaw.

Evo Johnson

I hop in my car, which isn't an easy thing to do with the bulge in my pants. Kenna is all consuming and my body reacted involuntarily.

I don't start the car right away. I watched her leave and witnessed the rust break away from the exterior every time the car jostled out of the parking long. Sitting there, I go over what just happened. She completely ignored an alpha's command. It didn't even faze her. My wolf was just as thrown, though he didn't like that I commanded someone he saw as *his*. He's never been possessive, so this new behavior of his leaves me baffled.

Normally, I don't use the alpha command on humans. It's considered immoral. Well-behaved shifters want them to have their own free will, and some even spend their nights protecting the frail species from vampires and rogues. I see it as taking away the right they've been given – to make choices on their own. But this female was beyond stubborn, so I tried the command to get my way. It didn't work. She didn't even give me a chance.

Whenever an alpha gives a command, those below me, humans included, obey it, even if it's against their will. So how in the world did it not even faze her? It should have. She isn't a wolf. The only way she could brush off a command was if she was my equal, which doesn't make any sense. It is impossible for her to be my equal.

I drum my fingers against my steering wheel. An equal would mean my mate, and wolf mates are destined to be other wolves. It's the way of our world. The order of species and survival ground so deep that somewhere out there, every wolf has a fated mate. Just one. One. Fated. Mate.

My wolf feels smug about it. Feels smug that this woman has me so flustered. At times like this, I think the creature knows more than I do. I wish he would just give me the answers, but that isn't his way. From time to time, he prefers to watch me suffer a little. We've always been on the same wavelength, but occasionally, he enjoys watching me struggle to figure things out on my own.

The crazy beast inside me shouldn't even recognize her – he never pays attention to humans, not to this extent. But this little female, he takes a great interest in.

I could scent her lust for me – could tell she was attracted to me – but she fought it time and time again, brushing me off as if I were a fly. It agitated my wolf that she didn't succumb to her lust. That she didn't let it take over and just come to me.

Jazz, a blonde female Cloven Pack member, is my go-to to scratch an itch. Dressed in nothing but what nature gave her, she came to me last night expecting our usual romp. I didn't let her get past my bedroom door before I turned her away. My wolf growled at the idea of that female in my bed and urged me to get rid of her. It didn't feel right to sleep with Jazz while Kenna consumed all my thoughts. It felt like I was betraying Kenna by even having Jazz knock in the first place. My wolf fully agreed. So this morning, I took all my bedding down to the laundry room and Kelsey washed them for me. I don't want Jazz's scent anywhere, especially where I lay my head.

Through my wet windshield, I watch as a married couple leaves the diner and leisurely strolls hand in hand to their car. Life would be so much easier if mates could be chosen by falling in love rather than forced by fate. Perhaps then I could give in to the urges and take Kenna home with me. Peruse this further than my own instinctual curiosity. But I know the human world isn't ready to discover us. They won't be able to accept it, and there's a good chance Kenna won't either.

I should have never asked her to breakfast.

That's all this is: Curiosity. I really need to figure out what this girl is, and more importantly, why I can't get her off my mind before she drives me and my pacing wolf crazy. Wolves don't lust after humans. It simply just doesn't happen and definitely not to me. I can't have a relationship with a human while alpha.

So, I'll figure her out and that'll be the end of it. Puzzle solved.

Forcing my mind to drift from Kenna to what Jackie had told us, I start my car and head toward the pack's territory.

I can't tell Kenna what Kenner really is. I'd bet my last dollar Kenna doesn't even know wolf shifters exist. Capturing Kenner to pin him to another crime is one thing, but having her discover there's another world out there is entirely different. And dangerous. He knew I was a wolf shifter the moment I walked into the interrogation room, and he knew I was an alpha. He also knew what Kenna was there for, because like all shifters, we have exceptional hearing. He could hear her behind the one-way glass, hear her unravel every truth and lie.

She's in far deeper than she realizes. I flip on the windshield wipers a bit too roughly as another bout of rain sprinkles across my window.

It might be a good idea to work this case behind her back.

I need to gather the entire pack and tell them about all of this. Since Kenner knows I'm also a wolf, there's a good chance he'll track down someone in the pack and retaliate simply for questioning him. He's alpha material himself.

If he wants to keep his secret about whatever he was doing with the abducted women, that would be enough incentive to silence us. I was lucky he didn't expose the shifter race right there in front of all those people. I grind my teeth. He could have easily done so just to throw me off my game.

I stiffen in the driver seat as the full repercussions of Kenna perusing this hits me in the gut. There's a serious possibility his attention could now be on Kenna. He knew she was there and aiding in this investigation. He saw her after the interrogation. He knows she's different, and, he could have just as easily waited around at the police station and watched my flirtatious interaction with her.

There's no way he didn't catch her scent and store it away for future retaliation, I think, cursing myself for a fool. The rogue is after women and I basically just handed him his next target.

I curse and thump my hand on the steering wheel. If I would have known Kenner was a wolf, I would have never involved any humans. I would have taken the pack to hunt him down before humans got involved.

It isn't like I can bring Kenna on pack territory, either. Even if she knew Chris Kenner might retaliate against her, I seriously doubt she would consider hiding on our territory. She seems determined to stay away from me, even if I know by scent that she finds me attractive. Besides, risk for discovery is just too great for the pack. We wouldn't be able to hide who we are.

The gravel under the tires crunch as I make my way down the pack's long driveway. The house is lit up with almost every light on in the house. I breathe a sigh of relief to the familiarity, having felt like I've been gone too long in the city.

Pulling up to the house, I mentally steel myself for the questioning I am going to get about Kenner. I know the pack will buck against the idea of having their alpha off pack territory, yet again protecting a human I seem to covet, while tracking down a woman-snatching rogue wolf.

My wolf doesn't see this situation as colorful as I do. To him, this is purely black and white. This is *his* Kenna to protect. That's how he sees her . . . as *his.*

I sigh, shutting off the engine. "It is going to be a long night," I murmur.

When I step through the front door and into the comfortably furnished living room, I hear Kelsey in the kitchen prepping for tomorrow's evening meal. The pack always eats together, and always at the alpha's table. The large kitchen is put to good use, and I'm grateful to Kelsey for stepping up and taking charge of it. We'd all starve otherwise.

Water bubbles loudly in a pot and a knife chops against a cutting board in a rhythmic beat.

Heading through the living room and into the dining room, I around the corner to the kitchen and I give her a nod when she smiles a greeting at me. She's at the large granite island chopping salad toppings.

A pile of sliced cucumbers towers at the edge of the wood cutting board. Her mate, Jeremy, lounges on a bar stool across from her, dipping freshly baked cookies in a mug of milk.

"How was the night out?" Jeremy asks before stuffing a cookie in his mouth.

Both he and his mate have shocking red hair, lean and tall, but that's where the similarities end. Jeremy features are harsher where Kelsey's are round and soft, and their personalities are the exact opposite, too.

"It was . . . informative." I scratch the side of my neck. "I'm calling a pack meeting. Think you can round everyone up and meet back here in ten minutes?"

Nodding, he hops off the stool, snatches two more cookies from their cooling rack, and heads out the dining room's sliding door to gather everyone. Though everyone has their own quarters, none of them connect internally to the other. Each quarter has their own entrance door accessible from the back lawn.

The oven beeps loudly in the spacious atmosphere. Kelsey wordlessly sets down the knife, wipes her hands on her apron, and relieves the oven from its sweet burdens. After sliding the cookies on their own drying rack, she piles the cooled ones on a large platter and places it in the center of the island.

"Thanks." I grab a cookie and take a chunk out of it. Not only is she a good cook, but a good baker, too.

"They're not all for you," she barks, as hot tempered as ever. "They're for everyone."

I grin at her. "Thanks for baking."

"Well if I don't do it, no one else will. You'd all starve."

I grunt my agreement, and when she turns her back to grab plastic containers for the cucumbers, I snatch another cookie.

"You like her, don't you," Kelsey states once she's facing me again. She leans her hip against the counter and piles the vegetables inside the container.

"Kenna?"

"Who else?"

I narrow my eyes. "I find her interesting."

This time it's Kelsey's turn to grunt. She sees right through me. "I think it's more than that."

"You know the rules, Kels."

She rolls her eyes. "No dating humans, yadda-yadda. The heart wants what the heart wants. There ain't no stopping that love bug, my friend."

I roll my neck, uncomfortable with the turn of conversation. I'm not ready to admit that my heart wants anything. It's impossible where Kenna and I are concerned.

"That still doesn't change the rules. Something that foolish could be catastrophic to our pack."

She thinks for a moment while nibbling on a cucumber's edge. "I suppose that's true. Still doesn't change anything though, does it?" I grunt again. "It's been pretty dull around here, anyway. We could use a little something-something to spice things up." Licking her bottom lip, she glances around the room and hushes her voice. "What are you going to do about Jazz if she finds out?"

I lean back on my stool and shrug. "There's nothing to tell."

She lifts a thin red eyebrow, smirking. "You're a damn fool. Speak of the devil, and she shall arrive."

Jazz strides around the corner, her heels echoing around the room as they hit the hardwood floor with each step. I can smell the dye from the new clothes she's wearing. She must've bought them today. A part of my mind always knew she dresses in such a way that doesn't belong to our lifestyle. High-heeled shoes, freshly dyed blonde hair, designer clothes, and a whole lot of makeup. It didn't fully come to my attention until now.

"Cookie?" Kelsey sweetly asks Jazz.

"Um, no." I didn't think she would. Jazz survives on celery sticks and almonds. Maybe even twigs for all I know. I don't understand why – wolves have high metabolisms.

Jazz wanders over to the stool next to mine and sits down in a posh sort of way. "I'll take some grapes though, Kelsey."

Kelsey stiffens and stares at her as if Jazz lost her mind.

Kelsey is a dominant wolf, but she isn't an alpha. Alpha or not, it's never a smart move to boss a dominant wolf around, or in this case, treat them like it's their job to serve. They'd sooner pluck eyes out with the sticks their wolves' play with than do as commanded by a lesser wolf.

"I'll be sure to peel them for you, too, princess," Kelsey snips before grabbing the grapes from the fridge and a bowl from the cupboard. Setting the bowl on the counter, she plucks grapes straight off the stem without washing them, and roughly slides the bowl back to Jazz.

I watch the entire ordeal with mild interest. Kelsey has a vengeful streak and is never afraid to put someone in their place. It often gets her into trouble, and once, it landed her in jail. She's a good-hearted person, but she's also a person to never piss off.

"What's the meeting for?" Jazz asks, popping a grape into her mouth.

Hiding my amusement to Kelsey's wicked grin, I stand up and walk to the other side of the island when Jazz tries to lean into me. I'm not comfortable with another female touching me right now. Not when my head is all confused.

"We need to talk about some things I've learned today. We'll discuss it when everyone arrives." Kelsey turns her body around so Jazz won't see her holding back a laugh for effectively being dismissed.

"Here they come," Kelsey says as the front door opens. Jovial laughter rings throughout the house as everyone makes their way into the kitchen and finds a seat at the island. The plate of cookies is quickly emptied, and crumbs are sprinkled across the counter.

Dyson and Flint, long time best friends, are holding a conversation with my sister Brenna. Ben listens to them with barely contained annoyance, his eyes on me expectantly. We're a small pack, but a proud and fierce one. My heart swells at the sight of everyone's smiles and gentle teasing.

Once Jeremy arrives, Ben clears his throat.

A deep breath, and I begin.

CHAPTER FOUR

Makenna Goldwin

I wipe the sweat running down my face with a towel that's wrapped around my neck, and deliver another series of fist-pummeling blows to the hanging, pathetic excuse for a punching bag. The *thump, thump, thump* mimics my rapidly rising heart rate and I relish heat increasing in my muscles. It is nearing midnight and my apartment complex's gym is completely empty, leaving me to my own thoughts.

The gym is shitty, to say the least. One treadmill, one bike, and one punching bag. I'm pretty sure the punching bag is older than I am. Its innards are being held inside by the duct tape I wrapped around it when I first moved here. The place smells like old socks, but there's nothing that can be done about that. The air freshener on the small window's ledge makes the place smell like a porta potty under a blazing summer sun.

Outside, sirens wail and cars honk, but I push the sound out and listen to my own labored breathing.

I work out most nights, knowing it's important to maintain a healthy body for my line of work. Occasionally, but not always, I have to use my merger stamina to keep myself safe. Not everyone loves it when a PI tracks them down. Learning to defend myself had become my number one priority over the past few years. Being bullied in the foster homes left me no choice as a teen, and chasing big men convinced me to continue as an adult. I don't like to rely on anyone else for my safety or otherwise. I can take care of myself.

Lie, my alter ego thinks.

"I can take care of myself," I grind out, pushing all my anger into my fists as I deliver a sequence of hits to the bag.

Working out tends to help me work off stress, which is what currently plagues my mind. My thoughts are a tangled web of Evo, Chris, and my investigation, flitting from one topic to another.

Evo is hell-bent to take me on a date, and yet, I've given him no outward indication that I'm attracted to him. I've tried to not let him see my gaze roam over his body, and carefully schooled my face when he made me weak at the knees with that intoxicating scent.

Not every human has exceptional senses like I do. Most humans don't even come close to my senses. I see sharper, hear better, move faster, and I can smell far better than the average Joe and Jane. It took me a long time as a child to realize how different I was from the others.

Chalking it down to good genetics, it still doesn't help when his scent can almost make me forget what I'm going to say or do, which is something I find appalling and unacceptable. I have to stay sharp and that's next to impossible with him standing so close, filling me with needs I don't have time for.

Lie, she thinks again.

That's the excuse I'm sticking to.

Maybe I should just screw this guy, get him out of my system, and get it over with. However, I don't truly believe he'll just disappear after a night in bed. That man is persistent, I'll give him that. And if I am being honest, I don't think one night of hot sex would be enough. Not for me, anyway. I'd stick like glue.

This time, she fully agrees with my thoughts.

The bag swings back too fast and I pivot swiftly, letting it hit me in the shoulder. I grunt upon the impact and steady the bag once more.

I'd want more and more of Evo. Something that would be completely against what I'm trying to accomplish – not having anyone I need to rely on or be centered to. I don't want someone who's looking for a relationship, because, well, I wouldn't know what to do with one. I'd fail at it. I've never had relationships. If and when I bring a guy home, which I rarely do, we never exchanged numbers because I make it clear from the beginning that I'm not interested in the white picket fences and wedding rings. Even though I am. Even though I envy those who have it.

Nope, I mentally tell myself, *no steamy sex with ex-agent hottie.* And that will just have to be that.

Chris Kenner is a whole other matter. I have no choice but to believe that Evo will leave the new discovery in my investigation between us and not blab to the nearest FBI agent he can find. I felt the truth in those words, so I shouldn't need to worry.

What I *am* worried about is where he's storing these women. Is he keeping them alive? Raping them? Selling them? Is Cassie even alive? There's no trail to follow. Women just disappear with absolutely no trace. If he's killing them, what's he doing with the bodies? There's been no reports of dead women. On a hopeless whim, I had checked before coming down here.

Wherever he's keeping them, it definitely has to be in a hidden facility. A place the FBI doesn't know about. Possibly abandoned. If he owns or rents any facility in his name, the FBI would have been all over that like white on rice. But the FBI has no concrete evidence that Kenner is even behind this, anyway. It's all speculation because he was seen talking to each missing woman, but not physically taking them.

Evo believes it though. He believes Kenner is the responsible party. The true question is, is Kenner working alone?

Delivering a few well-aimed kicks to the bag, I feel an emotion that isn't my own ripple over my skin – *anticipation* with a side of deep *hunger*, and not the hunger that comes with food.

I stop the bag's swing with one sore hand and stare at the wrinkled and worn duct tape, thinking. Listening. This kind of hunger is fed by evil. It's fed by someone who has every intention of doing dark deeds, and –

My heart skips a beat. There's someone watching me. I can feel the eyes pin prick the exposed skin on the back of my sweaty neck. From the window? Possibly.

Dabbing my forehead with the towel, I use my peripheral vision to glance around as I bend to grab my cell phone. I don't see anyone, but that's no surprise. In this part of town, it's always this dark at night. I know someone's there, though. I can feel them.

Could it be Kenner?

The clawing sensation forms inside my belly as *her* need to protect skyrockets. I ignore it, pushing her down, down, down, as if she's a physical thing inside me. Sanity tells me that the only thing here to protect me is myself. I remind her of this, even as my heart hammers inside my chest. It would not be a good moment to pass out on a nasty gym floor and have whoever is watching have their way with me.

The pin prick sensation abruptly disappears and I take reprieve for the blessing it is. I don't have a lot of time.

Hastily, I turn on the screen to my phone, make a split-second decision, and text the unsaved number. If this doesn't go in my favor, I'm going to need some backup. I'm going to need someone, anyone, to know I didn't just up and disappear, because I know, *I know*, that whoever is watching me is still near . . . waiting.

I press send and the phone chirps as the text is delivered. Hands shaking, I softly pad my way into the merger locker room. It's larger than the gym itself, and it has made me wonder why this part of the gym doesn't hold the equipment instead. Right now, I don't care though. It's wide open and just as absent of people as the gym is. There are no places to hide. There's no sound except the *drip, drip, drip* of the leaky sink, and the drum of blood whooshing in my ears. There is only the bench, the two bathroom stalls, and the metal lockers with no doors.

Making it look like I plan to rinse my face, I twist on the tap. The water sputters as I feel a rush of wind. I bend my knees to duck, successfully dodge the first blow, and spin around to face my attacker.

"What the fuck," I whisper and duck again to avoid the swinging arm aimed for my face.

The guy attacking me has blood-red eyes and hands formed like claws. His skin is so pale white that I can see the black snaky veins underneath, crawling under the surface like roots to a tree. He smells horrible, deathly, and dried blood is splattered across his cheek next to two large and gleaming fangs.

Before I can ponder what the hell this guy is – because he definitely isn't human – he catches me off guard and his sharp, pointed nails graze my shoulder. It enough, though. It's enough to tear the skin and hurt like hell.

Screaming in agony, I bump my back against the sink. The pain in my shoulder is nothing compared to what's going on inside me. My insides are clawed at harder, making me shake as I try to control the pain. My stomach feels like it's being peeled back layer by layer with a peeling knife. I clutch at it, digging my nails into my sweat slick abdomen. The feeling that I need to leave my skin and give in to my alter ego overwhelms me, and my muscles visibly quiver.

I spare a glance at my attacker just in time. He rushes me, a blur of speed. With every ounce of effort I have left, I bend and whirl around, tripping my freaky attacker's legs. He falls and slams into the sink. The sink cracks and water sprays.

Roaring, I grab his shirt and throw him at the lockers. With my extra strength, it isn't difficult. His head hits first, denting the metal, and then he drops to the bench, splintering the wood. I sway, my vision blurring, and clutch my abdomen once more. With the pain, it is getting harder to focus. Harder to breathe. *Harder to think*. I barely notice the water soaking my back.

He stands much faster than a normal human would've been able to after such a blow to the head. But even so, his body movements are quicker than they should be, almost a blur of speed. I swallow thickly. He's as fast as I am. I've never met anyone who could move as quickly as I can. The speed is unnerving, making me question which one of us is going to come out of this alive.

Being a fraction of a second slower than him causes me to be slammed into a wall. One second, he was baring his fangs by the lockers, and the next, I'm a foot off the ground, held up by my neck next to the broken sink. I kick my feet. I dig my nails into his hand. None of it helps.

Leaning closer, he hisses in my face as he tightens his grip.

My insides continue their brutal assault and I attempt to scream in agony. Not a sliver of air comes through my gaping mouth.

I'm going to die. I'm going to die.

Black spots start to form in my vision and blood pools heavy in my face. Overwhelmed by my own dilemma, I can't form the energy or concentration to find a way out of this. The tighter his hand grips, the weaker I become.

I am going to die.

Evo Johnson

Tapping a tune on my steering wheel, I make my way to Kenna's apartment. I had used my resources to find out where she lives, and I'm unimpressed by the location. It's not the best part of town for a single young woman to be living on her own. Hell, half the street lights don't work.

After an hour and a half of discussion, mainly surrounding Kenna, the pack and I agreed she needed to be moved. I'm going to take her to a hotel until we can decide where to hide her more permanently. At least until this is completely over and Kenner is dealt with. I'll have to find a way to explain to Kenna that she can't continue her investigation. She'll demand to know why and telling her we plan to end Kenner's existence because he is a rogue wolf shifter doesn't exactly roll off the tongue. I still haven't worked out my alternative excuse.

Once Kenner is dead, the pack agreed that Kenna should have no further contact with me. They have urged me to leave her alone. The risk of discovery is high if I continue to pursue her. The conversation had been interesting, though. Jazz is thoroughly pissed I'm showing any sort of affection toward another female, and she made no pains in hiding it. Kelsey and my sister Brenna were all for bringing Kenna to the pack territory, until Jeremy and Ben talked them out of it. I couldn't tell if they were serious, or if the idea of tormenting Jazz held greater interest to them. Either way, it doesn't matter. The rest of the pack voted against that idea, and they're right for doing so.

Since that conversation, my wolf has continued to growl and pace inside me. He doesn't like this plan and is seriously considering taking over so he can hunt down Kenna and protect her himself.

Damn animal. I tighten my grip on the wheel. He doesn't understand that Kenna is a human and doesn't know he exists. To him, she is the only important thing in the world. The only thing that matters.

My cell phone beeps, pulling me from my thoughts. Grabbing it from my dashboard, I smile at the screen. "Kenna," I whisper to the empty SUV.

The text says, *Help gym my apartment.*

I stare at the words for a moment, numbness replacing my thoughts, then the sudden spike of fear and adrenaline. My foot slams the pedal to the floor and I speed the last mile to Kenna's apartment, my heart thudding in my chest.

Is Kenner there? Is he attacking her? She must have had some kind of early warning of danger if she had the time to text.

What if I'm too late? *Shit. Shit. Shit!*

My wolf fights for control as I screech to a stop, yank my keys from the car, and bolt into the building. Upon entering, a sign points the way to the basement where it promises the gym will be. I hear the struggle with my sensitive hearing before I barge through the gym doors. My fear rises to an impossible level when I hear a guttural, otherworldly hiss.

Vampire.

I race to the locker room, bend the corner, and find Kenna pinned against the wall by the vampire. A wooden bench is collapsed and water sprays, creating puddles on the floor. A growl rips from my chest. I stalk forward, yank the vampire away from her, and throw him across the room. The vampire quickly recovers, stands, and hisses at me, saliva dripping from his fangs.

I let my wolf have some control, not fearing detection at this point, and partially shift. My hands extend into claws, my canines elongate, and I let out a fierce growl in return.

He darts toward me, a blur of speed, but I had anticipated the move. I've dealt with his kind before, the bane of every shifter's existence. They're quick, but predictable. Shoving my hand into his chest just before he reaches me, I grip my clawed nails around his cold, non-beating heart.

I wait to see if the vampire will surrender, snarling a warning in his face. I don't want to end his dead life if I don't have to. He hisses back and I feel his weight shift as if he is going to continue his assault. He has every intention of fighting to his second death.

Wrenching his heart out of his chest, I squeeze it and watch him disintegrate, flaking away into nothing but ash and sand. Seconds later, his black heart does the same inside my claw. I open my hand and let the ash float to the soaked floor.

My wolf fights for more control, angered that someone had attacked Kenna and worried that there may be more danger. I stand there struggling to contain and reassure him while working to regain my full human form. Kenna moans on the floor behind me and I close my eyes, willing the control. The beast settles as my heartbeats slows, soothed by the patterned splat of water, and my claws return to fingers.

Satisfied that I won't scare the human, I swivel and bend to Kenna. I frown at her writhing form. Doing a once over, I search for wounds or vampire bites, anything to explain her agony. But there isn't any. There's no blood or wounds besides the red ring around her neck and a sluggishly bleeding slash on her shoulder.

Attempting to uncurl her from her fetal position, I speak softly, "Kenna? Kenna, what is it? What hurts?"

Kenna moans and her body tightens, curling further in on itself. "My stomach. Something is clawing its way out." She lets out a scream and opens her eyes. "Please! Make it stop!"

My breath freezes. Her eyes are . . . green. Bright. Glowing with the wolf trying to get out. "Holy shit."

I take in a deep breath, tasting her wolf's scent that's now much stronger and more pronounced since Kenna is in such a vulnerable state. *Kenna's a wolf shifter*. How? How is this possible? She must have had her wolf buried deep – I've never once scented her wolf before now.

With quick thinking, I do the only thing I know to make the pain stop. I grab Kenna by the throat. Letting my wolf surface enough for my own eyes to glow, I wait for her wolf to recognize mine, and then growl a warning.

"Enough," I order Kenna's wolf.

Kenna stiffens under my grip, but her wolf understands the command and she slowly fades from Kenna's irises. When Kenna's brown eyes blink at me, I know she's back.

"What are you?" she whispers before fainting.

"I've been dying to ask you the same question," I mumble while gathering her up into my arms.

Standing, I look around and survey the damage. There's so much of it, the locker room in soggy ruin. Kenna had fought the vampire. Fought, and fought hard, but not hard enough. She would have died tonight, and that fear of death had probably been what made her wolf surface.

I make my way to my car with Kenna still out cold in my arms, lay her in the passenger seat, and climb into the driver side. Absentmindedly, I start the car and begin the drive back to pack territory. The whole drive there I wait for Kenna to show any signs of waking, but she never does. The car's quiet hum muffles her soft peaceful breathing.

My mind is having trouble comprehending that Kenna is a wolf, but the evidence is there. Now that I had smelled her –

I shake my head. It's unbelievable. I was sure she was something other than human before, but I still completely missed it. My wolf clearly didn't. I'm extremely annoyed with the creature for withholding such vital information.

It's easy to explain, though. She had buried her wolf so deep, it would have been next to impossible for another shifter to know. It's incredibly difficult to bury your wolf. She must constantly struggle with it. The thought alone has me and my wolf wincing in pain. It must have been agonizing for both of them. Why would she even bury her? Why would she do that to herself and her wolf? They're meant to live as one.

I look at the woman in question. A stray brown hair is curled around the rise of her cheek. I reach and remove it. Does Kenna belong to a pack? No, she couldn't have. No pack would allow a wolf to live on their own. Not unless they were banned. . .

No, I refuse to believe she was banned. Besides her quick wit, Kenna doesn't seem dangerous. Not dangerous enough to have a pack kick her out. I remember her folder and how it said she was found abandoned as a baby. The thought always makes my wolf growl. He doesn't understand how someone could abandon his Kenna. I can't either. It's unheard of to ban a baby shifter, so I seriously doubt that was the case here.

Where did Kenna come from? Surely, she knew I was a wolf. Why didn't she mention it? Wait . . . What if she doesn't know she's a wolf?

I pull into the pack house driveway, giving Ben's wolf a small wave as he runs beside the car. Parking, I stare at Kenna. Her clothes are soaked, but at least her wound has clotted. *What if she doesn't know she's a wolf?* I rub my hands over my face. Shit, this could get complicated fast.

Sparing Kenna one more glance, I exit the vehicle.

Ben, fully naked after shifting back to human form, is walking to my car across dewy grass which is reflecting the moon's beams. Nudity isn't a big deal with wolves, but I raise an eyebrow anyway. If Kenna wakes and sees a naked man outside the car, she'll lose her shit.

"Shit, Evo. Is that Kenna in the car?" he asks in disbelief, trying to peek into the dark interior. "I thought we all agreed she wasn't going to be brought back here."

"We did."

When he notices she isn't awake, he scowls. "What's wrong with her?"

I shove my hands into my pockets, cutting straight to the point. "She's a wolf, Ben. A shifter."

He slowly turns and looks at me with a doubtful expression, trying to see if he should take me seriously. Confusion scrunches his features when he realizes I'm not deceiving him. "How do you know she's a wolf?" He gestures toward my hand, streaked with black vampire blood. "Clearly something went down. Did she attack you? What the hell happened?"

"Someone sent a vampire after her. A young, inexperienced one, at that. After he flaked, I found Kenna struggling to keep her wolf in. Her eyes were glowing, and I could scent her wolf as she fought Kenna for control."

Exhausted from the day, I tug at the corner of my eyes with two fingertips. "Ben, I don't think she knows she's a wolf. It's the only conclusion I can come up with." He scoffs. "No really. Why else would she fight her wolf so hard? Her wolf was trying to protect her, but for some reason, Kenna fought the transformation. She feared the pain that it brought. When I commanded her wolf to back down, she asked me what I was before she fainted."

"She could be a banned wolf, Evo. A rogue. Maybe she played dumb so you wouldn't suspect what she was."

I shake my head. "I don't know, Ben. That just doesn't add up. She was abandoned as a baby. I doubt any pack would ban a pup." I clench my fists and close my eyes in shame. "I can't believe we thought she was a witch because of her gift."

Ben sucks in a breath and curses.

"What?" I ask him.

"Shit, Evo," Ben curses again. "Queen wolves are always gifted. She's not a witch." He flings out an arm. "She's a queen!"

Stunned, I stare at him. Slowly, I shift my weight to look at the woman in my passenger seat. My wolf is silent but mightily smug. One word describes what he's telling me as I look at Kenna. *Mine*.

Shit.

CHAPTER FIVE

Makenna Goldwin

Snuggling in deeper, I take a deep whiff of the soft fabric rubbing against the bridge of my nose. This bed is so soft and warm. I'm cocooned in heavy blankets, my head resting on several plush, but firm, pillows. It's heavenly. Rich. So unlike my –

I still my movements.

This does not smell like my bed. This does not feel like my bed. The familiar sounds of my apartment in the middle of the city are absent to my ears. Instead, birds tweet from a nearby window that's letting in a large amount of sunlight.

I desperately search my mind of where I last crashed. Fear invades me and *she* claws at my insides as the memories flood my mind. Did the fanged man take me?

Bolting upright, I take in my surroundings with wild eyes. The scent is familiar – *Evo*, my memory tells me. I'm in Evo's bedroom. I grip the sheets tightly. Having no memory of getting here, I search my mind again.

I had sent him a text telling him I needed help. I remember him pulling the creepy guy off me. Did the creep really have red eyes? No, I had to have imagined that. I remember pain, lots and lots of pain, as *she* fought to get out – to surface and protect like she always does whenever I have the least bit of anxiety.

I remember Evo and his eyes. *His eyes.*

Gasping, I fly out of the bed and bump into the nightstand. I fumble to keep the jostled, rocking lamp from tipping over and breaking. His eyes were glowing green. He was a monster, just like the red-eyed creep.

"No, no, no, no, no," I whisper, a hand over my mouth. "This is just a really bad dream. That's all, Kenna. Pull yourself together. It was all a bad dream."

Hearing footsteps approach the bedroom door, I search for something I can use to defend myself. If I am in Evo's home, he had fought off my attacker, which meant he was stronger than him. Crazier than him. More of a beast than him.

Panic seizes me, roots me to my spot, as the door opens and I still have no weapon.

"Knock, knock," a deep rumbling voices calls. "You awake?"

Evo sticks his blond head in the doorway. He takes in my panicked appearance and his eyes grow a fraction wider.

Striding over to me with purposeful steps, his irises begin to glow the green I remembered. I clutch my stomach against the clawing sensation. Before I can back away or run, he has me collared by the throat, the tip of his nose inches from mine.

"Relax," he demands. I shake my head. "Relax," he says softer. "I won't hurt you. You're safe, Kenna. Do you hear me? You're safe."

His words are weighted, heavy with a command that's almost physical. The pain in my stomach subsides, and even though my fear still lingers in the background, my breathing eases. My alter ego, however, doesn't fear him. She finds comfort in him.

I watch his eyes retreat back to their normal blue color as he eases his grip, softly rubbing his thumb back and forth on my neck. Drifting his hand to my frightened face, he rubs the back of his fingers over my cheek.

"Better?" Evo whispers.

I clear my throat, trying to get rid of the lump that has formed there. *Grow some balls, Kenna*, I scold myself. *Buck up and grow some balls.*

Feeling his compassionate emotions run over my skin helps relax me further. Rationality tells me there is no reason to fear him when his emotions aren't aggressive.

I wiggle my fingers, a repetitive soothing motion that reminds me I have a sliver of control. When I feel I can respond, I say the first thing that pops out of my mouth. "What the fuck is going on?" I meant for it to come out with anger and aggression but instead, it comes out weak and pitchy.

A serious expression rearranges his face and he drops his hand to his side. "Why are you suppressing her, Kenna?"

I frown. Who am I suppressing? "What? That's not what I asked, Evo; if that's really your name. What am I doing here? Where is here? What is going on? Who *are* you?"

Running a hand through his hair, he sighs, resolved to the fact that I'm not going to answer his question just yet. Not that I have any idea what he is talking about.

"I'm still me. My name is still Evo Johnson. I brought you to my territory for your safety and protection. After I killed the vampire, I didn't —"

I cut him off with my screech, "A vampire? That *thing* was a fucking vampire?"

He looks at me like I'm a frightened little bird, keeping his words and movements slow and reassuring to be sure I don't fly off at the first sign of danger. "Yes. Red eyes, death stench, fangs, and all. That was a vampire and a new turn at that. Someone had sent him to kill you."

"Kill me?"

A nod. "That's what most vampires do. They're super-naturals for hire. If there's blood involved, they couldn't care less what crime they're committing or whose life they're ending. Tonight, that life was supposed to be yours."

My hysterical laugh falls to a frown. "Let's just say I believe there are vampires roaming the streets and they're hirable criminals. What could someone possibly gain from taking me out? I haven't exactly pissed in anyone's Cheerios, lately."

Evo's eyebrows shoot up, like this should be an obvious answer.

I think about it for a minute, and then sigh when it hits me. "Chris Kenner. He saw me as he was leaving the interrogation room, and now I'm investigating one of the women he most likely took." I glance away and to the window, peering at the green grass below. "His emotions and state of mind weren't exactly friendly toward me the other night. Damn it, I knew he had heard me from the observation room. Wait, so . . . does this make him a vampire, too? He wasn't exactly all fangy. Shit! Is he drinking those missing women's blood?"

"He's not a vampire," Evo says while taking a seat on the edge of his bed, watching my hysterics with interest.

"But he's hiring them?" I rub my arms. "What is Kenner doing hiring a monster? I can't imagine any human wanting to work with *something* who looked like that. Where would someone even find a vampire to hire? It's not like they're in the phonebook under blood-sucking hitmen."

Taking a few steps back, I sink into a plush reclining chair and put my head in my hands. Everything in his room is plush and expensive looking, from the thick pushed-back curtains to the cream-colored chairs that make a cozy seating area. If I were here under different circumstances, I'd be enjoying this extremely soft chair with chips scattered across my breasts.

I must be dreaming. "Vampires aren't real. Monsters aren't real. And people, no matter how insane they are, don't go out and hire creatures of the night to assassinate private investigators because they tattled on you for lying."

"Kenner isn't human, Kenna. He is what I am. What you and I are."

Silence – a taut pause. "Come again?"

He scratches at the stubble along his jaw. "You really don't know who you are?"

My spine straightens as I glare at him. "Are you from crazy town? Do you hear yourself?"

In answer, he pinches the bridge of his nose.

"*You really don't know who you are?*" I mock. "I'm human. Normal. I seem to be the only normal person around. It's me who should be asking who you are!"

"That's not what I was trying to ask. Listen to me." He stands. The bed frame squeaks and he walks toward the chair, kneeling in front of me on his plush white rug. I refuse to shrink back, even if this guy is just as much of a loon as I am starting to think he is. "Do you know *what* you are, Kenna?"

I frown again. It sounds like the same question to me. "Um . . . human," I say as I pat myself down in a dramatic gesture. "A little bitchy, and possibly insane because I happen to be stuck in some kind of nightmare right now, but yeah, I'm pretty sure I'm human."

His sympathy washes over my skin, causing me to bristle like an offended cat. Sympathy is never an emotion I like to feel coming from others. Especially if it is directed toward me. It makes me uncomfortable and the last thing I want is someone else's charity.

"So, I was right. You don't know." He stands up. I watch him walk the span of his room and then back again. Once he reaches me, he looks back into my eyes. "Do you remember what happened last night? That pain you felt?"

"Yes," I nod with certainty. "It's a frequent occurrence for me. They're called panic attacks. Loads of people get them. You should research it."

His jaw ticks at my flippant attitude. I square my shoulders, showing him just how crazy this all is and just how sane I am while surrounded by, what seems to be, a world full of ill-mannered fruit loops.

"No, Kenna. Those are not panic attacks. When I looked into your eyes before you fainted, I saw her staring back at me."

"Come again?"

"You are not human, Kenna!" He flings his arms, the muscles rippling like shifting rocks. "You never have been. That gift you have? Where you can tell what others are feeling? That's rare among your race . . . *our* race. That gift makes you a queen."

I laugh out loud and survey around the room for a crown. "A queen? Of what? Have you lost your ever-loving mind?"

He shakes his head and lowers his voice. "You're a wolf shifter. Like me. Like Kenner."

I cock my head to the side. I must not have heard that right. "Wolf . . . shifter. Are you telling me that you . . . that I . . . am a werewolf?" I chortle, unable to hold it back. "Look, I think I'd be the first to know if my extra-curricular activities included howling at the moon."

"Damn it, Kenna," he growls. "You are unbelievably stubborn. This is not a game. This is not a trick. I'm telling you the damn truth! Will you stop being so ignorant and just feel what I'm feeling?"

My giggle fit subsides, and I look at the angry, burly man in front of me. Feeling his waves of emotion reach me, I feel . . . a hint of *lust*, *annoyance,* and *anger*, and . . . *truth*. I gulp and shrink into the recliner. "Shit."

He bobs his head, relieved I am finally comprehending, and moves to sit back on the bed.

I lean back in the chair, overwhelmed. "So . . . I'm part wolf, part human? No, wait. I was born a human but was infected or something and became part wolf?" Realization hits me. "Wait. I hate to burst your bubble, Evo, but I've never sprouted fur, walked around on all fours, or held any fascination with the moon. I think you have it wrong – you're wrong. You may believe you're right, but you're not. I'm human."

"I'm not wrong," he states firmly.

"You are," I counter.

His agitation is becoming smothering. "The panic attacks – they aren't panic attacks. I can understand how you might think so, but from first-hand experience, that clawing sensation is actually your wolf fighting for the surface. Don't you feel her inside you?" Giving me pause to let that sink in, he continues, "Being a wolf shifter doesn't happen because you've been infected with some kind of virus. We're born this way – an entirely different species. We aren't werewolves – we're not held by the moon, and we don't eat people every full moon because we can't control our urges. Shifting happens at will. We co-exist with the animal inside us."

"Co-exist," I murmur, just to hear the word on my own tongue.

96

He shakes his head. "I'm not entirely sure how you survived this long and kept your sanity. I'm not even sure how you haven't discovered what you are simply by accident. Do you feel something there? Like an extended presence?"

I reluctantly nod. I always thought I was insane. That something was mentally wrong with me. It would fit if that meant my alter ego wasn't some kind of defect with my brain, but instead, my wolf.

A part of me desperately wants this to be true. That I am, in some way, normal to some corner of the world. If I am a wolf shifter, it means I belong somewhere.

I think about that. If wolves are born, then it would stand to reason it's genetic. I don't have a clue who my parents are, so how could I possibly have known this thing inside me is actually my wolf. If I had no one there to guide me and say otherwise, how could I think differently?

When I was younger and in the foster system, I bounced around from family to family. When the first family thought I was crazy, they sent me to a shrink who agreed with their search-engine diagnosis and gave me medicine in hopes of correcting it.

The rest of the foster families didn't like that they had to take me to see a shrink, nor the inconvenience of making sure I took my pills. They always told me it cost too much money, or I took too much of their time away from the other foster kids. I never even got the chance to be adopted. No one wanted a kid who was an emotional mess.

With my gift, I spent a great deal of time trying to decipher between my own emotions, other people's emotions, and her emotions. It was confusing as a child and I spent a great deal of time crying or being doused with medicine. When I was old enough, I decided to live on my own thinking it would be easier. It's why I preferred to be alone. But ever since I can remember, I've been on those pills.

I tell Evo all this, my voice seemingly far away. He listens patiently until my story comes to a close. "I thought I had some kind of alter ego inside me, like multi-personality disorder or something. To counteract my crazy, I've been taking pills to cope."

Evo growls at me and his eyes flash green.

I cock my head. "How do you do that? Why do your eyes glow green?"

"I told you. It can happen when your wolf lunges to the surface. I've seen you do it twice now."

Surprised, I say, "Really? I've never seen my eyes do anything like that. When did you see them glow?"

"Once, after I killed the vampire, and another when I came through this door." He points toward his bedroom door.

"Oh. Right. Okay." I put that nugget of information to the side for further evaluation later. "Well, anyway, I take the pills, it knocks me out, and the pain and migraines are gone the next day. At least, until I get worked up again."

Another taut pause to allow me to sort myself out. "That would make sense. If I had a wolf inside me . . . It is inside me, right?" At his nod, I continue, "Right, okay, so, with my wolf inside me, I can only imagine that she would want to surface, causing me to shift or whatever, so she can defend me, whether there is any real danger or not. Right?" I look at him for confirmation.

"Right." Evo nods. "That's normal. It's part of their nature – to defend their human half when we aren't capable, or the threat is too great."

"I always thought I was insane or something," I repeat in a mumble.

He smiles again, clearly satisfied that I am finally believing him. "What do you feel right now? Close your eyes and tell me what she's feeling."

I do as he asks, simply because I am curious. "Protected. Curious. Possessive." I frown. "She feels possessive?" I question while opening my eyes to look at him, only to find his smile growing wider. "What? What does that mean?"

He coughs and scratches his eyebrow. I don't need to feel his emotion to be able to tell this next topic is going to be an uncomfortable one. "Spit it out, Evo."

"Wolves have mates."

"Like friends? Or lovers? What kind of mates are we talking about here?"

"Lovers. Wolves mate for life. There is only one other wolf shifter in the world who would be compatible with another. We think it all comes down to nature. Biologically a perfect match, it guarantees children."

"That makes sense, I suppose. I've heard of some animals mating for life. A little unfair that it's not by choice, but it sounds slightly romantic, I suppose."

Evo steeples his fingers under his chin and rests his elbows on his knees. "Once they find their mate, the female is able to have pups. The mating is on a mystical level. Once a mating bond is fully formed, the mated pair can feel what the other feels, have pups, even communicate telepathically if it's a strong mated pair. Coupling with someone other than their mate won't ever produce any of those things."

"What does any of this have to do with my wolf," that just feels weird to say out loud, "feeling possessive."

"Mates recognize each other." His cheeks redden in a bright blush. "Usually, it's the wolves who recognize the signs first. Everything about the other is hypnotizing to them. Their scent, their looks, and their personality. It's all attractive to them. When a wolf recognizes their mate, the urge to have sex is strong because it would start the mating process."

Impatient, I snip, "My light bulb still isn't going off."

He sighs again. The man has the patience of a saint. "My wolf also feels possessive. Possessive of you, Kenna." He meets my eyes, jaw ticking as his embarrassed vibes settle across my skin. "You've been the only thing on my mind since the police station. Your scent knocks me off my feet, your strength gives me pride, and my dreams have been extremely . . . vivid. My wolf thinks of you as his."

When I don't respond he says the three words I feared he would, "You're my mate."

CHAPTER SIX

Makenna Goldwin

The birds are calming as I sit here staring at the edge of the pond. It's surrounded by a thick mossy forest, and across its smooth glassy surface, deep green lily pads bob. I had found it on Evo's property. Or 'territory,' as he calls it.

On the other side, birds and ducks peck the ground while occasionally eyeing me with suspicion. I perch on top of a large rock, trying to use the stillness of the water to relax my inner turmoil. It's a perfect place to sit and mull over what I've just learned. *A perfect spot to hide.*

I had run from Evo's room, catching glimpses of several people out on the property. They had stopped what they were doing and watched me as I fled into the forest behind Evo's giant mansion. I didn't know where I was going, but at the time, it didn't matter. I found solace in the shadows of the trees as soon as they folded me away from the sun and watchful eyes.

This is what I have feared all my adult life. This is what I don't want and what I've completely avoided. While everyone around me is settling down, getting married, and having kids, I want nothing to do with it. Because I'll fail at it. I'll be a disappointment. I don't want to have to rely on anyone and I sure don't want to have anyone rely on me. To be told I'm a part of a half wolf, half human species, with a destined mate to boot, I understandably bolted. Evo hadn't tried to stop me, either. Predestined commitment for life sounds more frightening than the vampire assassin.

It's not that I don't feel the pull to Evo. I have from the very start. It is exactly as he described – strong and all consuming. I know he feels the same because I can *feel* it. He finds me attractive and suitable, but does he find *me* attractive? My soul, or whatever? Or is this just nature and the predestined bond?

I chuck a pebble in the pond and it plunks into the water, sending ripples across the surface and disrupting the lily pads. Ducks take flight, seeing me as a sure threat.

People can't just go around telling oblivious strangers that from this day forward, you will want me and only me. How am I supposed to handle this on top of discovering I'm also a wolf shifter?

All my life, I never thought I was anything more than a human. A damaged human, but still a human, nonetheless. Then along comes a creepy wolf-man who abducted people, a hot ex-FBI agent who also is a wolf, and a serial killer assassin who does favors for blood. All are part of a supernatural world, and all of a sudden, I'm told I'm from this nightmarish reality, too.

If I hadn't seen the evidence for myself . . .

Feeling the truth in his words had made it easier to accept. But do I really want this? Do I plan to leave my human life and become mated to the man I left behind in the mansion?

I comb a hand through my hair and tug at the roots. When I ran, I could feel his *hurt* at my rejection. It had done something to me as I dashed down the steps. For just a moment, his feelings had made me hesitate, reconsider. I haven't hesitated over a man. Ever.

It's like this is entirely out of my control – this attraction and pull I have toward Evo. I have no choice in the matter. It's like a prearranged marriage, but this time, Mother Nature is the one doing the arranging. A biological chemistry that's set in stone and woven through DNA.

The urge to return to him is strong. I want to go back, because something inside of me is restless and disappointed. *My wolf*, I realize. She wants me to seek her mate. Our mate. She doesn't approve of my reluctance.

I don't know how intelligent my wolf is, but she's not seeing the bigger picture here. If I'm going to do this, if I'm going to consider the idea of giving in and settling down, I want to do it because I want to.

Not because nature and supernatural biology told me so. If I'm going to spend the rest of my life with someone, I want to actually be in love. I don't feel that yet. Hell, I probably wouldn't know what love is even if it smacked me in the face. Being able to feel his emotions, I know he doesn't love me, either.

My wolf fills with anticipation from my thoughts. It swirls around my insides and nudges me in my mind. She wants me to give it a shot. To try. Maybe she's right.

I turn my head as I hear soft footsteps headed in my direction. A dark-haired, well-built man – though not as well built as Evo – approaches, twigs crunching underfoot. He sits down next to me, leans forward, and crosses his arms over his knees to study the cloud's reflection in the pond. He was one of the first people I had seen when I dashed from the house. I watch him until he speaks, knowing he means me no harm.

"You must be the alpha's mate," he murmurs, tone deep and gravelly. I bristle, but he presses on. "I'm Ben, Evo's beta. The pack lives here on the territory, if you didn't notice already."

"I noticed," I say reluctantly.

At the time, I didn't really wonder why there were people on his property, but I also didn't know Evo was alpha. That is a tiny shock to my system. I know what that means – he is responsible for everyone in the pack. I don't know how I feel about that.

"I saw you run from the house." Ben angles his head toward me. He holds out his hand for me to shake. I take it. "I heard Evo dropped a bomb on you. How are you handling it?"

I turn my gaze back to the pond. A bomb is accurate. He dropped that bomb and my emotions exploded into the air and scattered around in a heap of a mess.

I remain silent until something pops into my head. "What does it mean to be a queen wolf?"

A soft exhale mixes with a gentle breeze before he says, "Queen wolves are gifted and very dominant. They have one extra sense the other wolves do not. They're rare. So rare, that I've never met one before. Their strength and speed are unmatched to others, with only one exception – their mate."

"Oh?"

"It is said that once they find their mate and allow the mating process begin, their mate will get to share the queen's gift."

"And you think I'm a queen." It isn't a question, but rather a statement. He feels the need to answer anyway.

"I don't *think* you are one. I *know* you are."

I adjust my seat and continue to overlook the pond, digesting what he revealed. A leaf drops into the water and I watch as the ripples travel to the rocks.

I've never thought that feeling others' emotions was a gift. As a child, I felt it was a curse. Knowing how unwanted I was, it was always a blow to the heart. It's made me shy away from accepting anyone in my life. I'm unable to connect because I can feel when I'm not wanted – by my foster families, friends, or lovers. When they don't know how to handle me, it upsets them, and my foster families would call the agency and have me rehomed. Eventually, I grew thicker skin and moved on from the foster system, using my curse to make a living.

It still would be nice not to be plagued with my . . . gift. Sometimes, I want to be lied to. To be ignorant of the truth. They say ignorance is bliss. I wouldn't know anything about that.

"Do you have a mate?" I ask him, peeking sidelong.

The corner of his lips tilts up. "Not yet."

We both remain silent, content on watching birds bicker in a tree before Ben speaks. "It must have been hard, not knowing what you are. You spent years thinking you're human and suppressing the other half." He meets my gaze for a brief moment. "You've spent your entire life fighting her and you didn't even know it. The strength you've shown is astonishing, but I can't imagine your life has been easy."

I scoff. "Strength? I don't exactly see it that way."

"I know. But Evo does. He's always known who and what he is. Last night, he learned that not only has he found his mate – the person he's spent his whole life waiting for – but he's found his other half.

His other soul, if you will." He rubs his hands along his jeans, uncomfortable with the depth of the conversation. "It may not feel that way for you, but it feels that way for him. He's waited a long time, just for you. Hell, the whole pack has been waiting for him to find his mate, and truth be told, we're happy you're here." With that, he gets up and brushes his pants off.

"You're leaving?"

"Duties." He grins and touches my shoulder. "I hope you plan to stay. We could use someone like you in our pack. From what I hear, you're quite the spitfire. You would liven things up."

I watch him pick his way through the trees until my neck strains with the effort. When he puts it like that, I can see why Evo felt rejected by my fleeing. If the roles were reversed – if I wasn't so determined to refuse to get close to anyone – I'd feel exactly the same way. It doesn't make me feel different about wanting to be loved, though.

From Ben, I could feel that he was truthfully glad that I was here. I could feel that he wanted me to stay and even believed I would. That just isn't something I am sure of. I know nothing about this life.

Even if I decide to give this a shot, what will I do about my job and clients? Will this change my life so drastically? Will I still be able to lead a somewhat normal life? Or will I just not be . . . me . . . anymore. When something changes in your life that's so drastic, it's harder to accept a new future than the one you had already mapped out. *But Evo will understand me*, a little voice in my head says. *I am what he is.*

As soon as I know Ben is long gone, I make my way back. Now, standing at the back of the white mansion, I stare at several doors I hadn't noticed before. Why would the back of a mansion need so many exits? And which one do I choose to get back inside?

"A little odd looking the first time you see it, isn't it?" a sweet voice says. I glance over as a woman comes to stand next to me, shading her eyes against the bright mid-morning sun and glancing at the sprawling patio. My age and my height, her shoulder length blonde hair shifts in the breeze. And her features . . . If I didn't know any better, she could easily be Evo's sister.

Turning toward me, she smiles brightly and sticks out her hand. "I'm Brenna, Evo's sister. Everyone calls me Bre. Well, except for my brother." Her nose crinkles in distaste for her given name.

Batta-bing batta-boom.

"Kenna." I shake her hand. It's soft, warmer than my own which had grown chilly next to the pond.

"I know." When I look taken aback, she supplies me with answers. "We had a pack meeting last night. Evo told us about you."

"I see."

"Oh, I hope you don't take that the wrong way. We don't keep many secrets here. Gossip tends to spread like wildfire, but it's prudent that we are all aware of circumstances and people who could involve us as a whole."

I nod my understanding. If a pack resembles a family of sorts, it makes sense to keep the members informed.

"So, how many of you are there?"

"Including myself, there are eight of us. There used to be a lot more, but they left to join another pack when Evo became alpha."

"They didn't want Evo to be their alpha?" I question. He seems like a good guy to me. Pushy, but caring and warm.

"Oh no. Everyone loved and thanked Evo for challenging and killing our father, the old alpha. But when the challenge was over and we were all free, many wanted to leave to get away from the memories." I cock an eyebrow and she smiles sadly. "It's quite common for wolves to find a new sanctuary when they're finally free of a controlling and abusive alpha. They respected Evo and his new position, but they wanted to start a new life. Evo never judged them for it."

I curse under my breath and put my hands on my hips, glaring at the mansion accusingly as if it's Evo himself.

"Oh." Realization hits her and she bites at the inside of her cheek. "My brother didn't tell you any of that, did he?"

I shake my head, both in answer and exasperated.

Evo killed his father. *His father.* I wonder what kind of man his father was that Evo felt the need to challenge and kill him. That must have felt terrible, killing his own father. Unless his dad deserved it, but I have no idea what he would have done to deserve to die. Bre had said abusive. How far did the man go? I'm not entirely sure I want the answer.

Thinking about Evo gives me butterflies and I fidget nervously. As scared as I feel, I am going to have to talk to him soon. We need to clear the air and I really want to ask him about all this. Bre and Evo may be siblings, but I still feel his father's death is his story to tell.

The thought of getting to know Evo is intriguing, though. As the alpha of this pack, he has to be a strong guy, mentally as well as physically. Just the way Bre talks about him, there is so much love in her voice, eyes, and emotion. Ben is the same way. They respect him. He had to have done something to gain their respect.

I gesture at the behemoth in front of us, its shadows stretching across the neatly trimmed lawn. "So, why are all these doors on the back of the mansion?"

"It's not really a mansion. It just looks that way from the outside for the humans' sake. The only entrance on the front is to the alpha's quarters. That way, if any humans come knocking, they will just assume it's Evo's house and not a house for several people. Discretion and all that." Extending out her arm, she points. "Each one of those doors is an entrance to a living quarter. Each wolf, or mated pair, gets their own quarter."

"I see." I scratch the back of my neck. "Well, actually, no, I don't. Why doesn't everyone just live in their own house? Why is everyone living on the same property?"

She gives me a small smile. "I know it must seem odd to you. Frankly, I don't know how you did it, living all on your own. Most wolves go rogue without the comfort of a pack nearby. Wolf packs, real wolf packs, live in a den, or something similar, together. Humans live in houses separate from each other. Doing it this way appeases both sides of our needs. To have space, but also comfort and protection. Our wolves crave touch and comfort, while our human side craves independence."

I nod. "Sure."

"Chris Kenner," she begins, abruptly changing the subject. When I look at her, surprised she knows that name, she reminds me with a knowing expression. "Pack meeting," she explains. "He's probably insane."

"Oh, he's insane alright," I mutter.

"Like I said, most wolves who go rogue eventually go insane. They become more animal than human, and when that happens, their brain warps in odd ways." She twists her lips and shivers. "It's likely that whatever he is doing with the women he's abducting feels right in his mind. He might understand right from wrong, but most likely, his animal has taken over. Sometimes nature isn't so cut and dry."

I rub my arms, unsettled. Kenner's cold blue eyes surface in my mind's eye and chip away at my resolve. What makes me so different than him? Because I'm a queen? I was alone for years and I didn't lose my humanity. Maybe it's because I grew up without comfort of any kind. I grew accustomed to it. I learned to cope from the day I was abandoned. I also fought my wolf from day one, thinking she was a symptom of some medical disorder. Even now, as I think about how much I fought my nature and her right to be acknowledged, I can feel her understanding. She knows I meant no harm because I didn't know she existed. And now, she's satisfied that I now fully accept she exists.

I don't know Kenner's history or why he's not in a pack, but I have a feeling he's far past help.

"What do you think he's doing with them? The women, I mean."

Her lips form a hard line. "If I'm right and his animal has taken over, it's likely those people are dead. Either his wolf killed them for sport, or he ate them on instinct."

My own rage and disgust mirror that of Bre's. Cassie is likely dead. How am I going to tell Johanna? I will need to bring her concrete evidence before I can drop that bomb. She won't accept it, otherwise. That means I'll have to find Kenner, possibly catch him in the act, or at least find where he's taking them.

In the light of things, I find it likely he sent a vampire to kill me after all. He would want to cover his tracks before anyone had the chance to dig them up. I sigh. *I'm the loose end, and so is Evo.*

"We need to find that bastard. Jail won't be enough. I'm gonna kill him."

Shocked by my venomous tone, Bre's eyes widen, and then she averts her gaze to her polished toes nestled in the grass. I feel her submission like it is an emotion. I can *feel* my wolf accepting and respecting it, too. And, among it all, I can feel her pride in my statement.

"You okay, Bre?"

She looks up at me. "Do me a favor?"

"Sure."

"Make it hurt."

I smile.

CHAPTER SEVEN

Evo Johnson

In my office, flipping through the pack budget, I feel some relief to the ache in my chest which had settled heavily from Kenna's rejection. We're finally above the red line in our savings, an accomplishment that had always seemed too far to grasp. My father, the bastard, had drained it dry and then some.

If they're able, each member of the pack, besides the alpha and beta, are required to have a job. A small percentage of their salaries normally go to our savings, but since we're in such debt, each member has been chipping in extra. I never asked them to, but they are all determined to help the pack out after my father destroyed it.

It gives me comfort to know that I'm not taking all their hard-earned money and depositing it in the pack bank account, like some other alpha's require.

I want to be sure they have their own money to do what they wish with it. The pack's bank account should only be there to take care of the roof over our heads, the land that surrounds us, and other minor necessities. My father had taken that for granted.

I lean back in my office chair and pop my neck.

Though he's gone, things haven't exactly been lively around here. Everyone is still mentally healing, and there's only one mated pair in the pack. Then there is me, who found my mate but was rejected by her.

The rejection stings more than I thought possible. I knew she would fight our mating. A sane person would. She's completely dependent on herself and seems to have been for a very long time.

She has no family, no real friends, and her job is her life. Not to mention she thought she was only human before today. I knew she would struggle trying to fit into a world she didn't know existed, but it never occurred to me that she might reject me by literally running out the door.

I just hope like hell she won't reject the pack as her own. She needs the pack, not just for the comfort it brings, but for her safety.

A knock sounds on my office door and I suppress a groan. I already heard someone approaching and I could tell who it was by scent and the noise of her heels. It was a conversation I knew would be had, eventually.

"Yeah?" I answer.

The door soundlessly swings open and Jazz sways in, twirling a strand of long gold hair around a finger. She smiles at me seductively, and makes her way to sit on the edge of my disorganized oak desk.

"What can I do for you, Jazz?" My tone is flat, bored. I know why she is here. If she's looking for someone to confide in, everyone knows that's Ben's job. She is here for either attention or sex. It's what she always wants.

She picks up my pencil and taps her chin with it. I flex my jaw, annoyed. For months, she's been hinting at wanting more than our occasional romp. No matter how many times I tell her I'm not interested, she still presses.

"I wanted to see if you were okay," she eventually says, lilted with false sympathy.

"What?"

"I heard you brought back that girl you were talking about last night, and then I saw her running from the house and into the woods." Invading my space, she strokes her hand across my shoulder and continues, "Did you two have a fight?"

I keep my posture confident and unapproachable. It is never wise to move away from a wolf if you're the alpha, especially a submissive wolf like Jazz. It is their job to move out of your space if they aren't wanted. I need to make it clearer to Jazz that our relationship, sexual in its nature, is at an end.

"Makenna is my mate and she's struggling with it. She'll come around."

Confusion sweeps over her face. "But that's not –"

"Possible?" I cut her off. "She's not human. She's a wolf shifter who only discovered everything this morning when she and I discussed it. She fled because she's confused and overwhelmed." If Jazz had bothered to crawl out of bed for our impromptu meeting while Kenna slept, she would have known.

Jazz thinks about it for a second, and then trails small circles below my collar bone. "Surely I can keep you company until she comes around." The look on Jazz's face makes it seem like she wishes Kenna will never come around, but I don't think she would pose a threat to my mate. Most shifters step aside if a wolf they're fooling around with finds their mate.

Thinking of ways to let her down gently, she takes my silence as an opportunity to sit on my lap. Again, I don't move, fully intending to make her get out of my personal space with verbal commands.

"Jazz, you need to get off."

She ignores me and rubs her cheek against mine. It is a sign of affection reserved for wolves who are more than just friends.

"She rejected you or she'd be here. Let me help make that pain go away."

"Jazz –" A gasp at the door cuts me off. We both look up. Grasping the door handle tightly, Kenna stands, shocked, in the doorway.

"Shit," I say before Kenna turns and marches down the hall. I stand up and Jazz lands with a thud on the floor. I start to make my way after Kenna, intending to explain.

"Wait, Evo!" Jazz screeches.

I whirl around, lacing the alpha's command into my voice. I normally don't do that to my wolves, but Jazz needs to understand I am out of patience for her continued antics. She hurt my mate. My wolf is growling and pacing inside me, completely furious I let this female touch me in the first place.

"No!" I slice a hand through the air. "Let's get one thing straight, Jazz. There will be no you and me anymore. Kenna is my mate and I have every intention of mating her. Get out of my office and go back to your own quarters. Do not come back here looking to seek my comfort again."

Eyes wide from my command, she lowers her head in submission. Satisfied that the message was received, I turn to hunt down my mate.

Makenna Goldwin

Marching out of Evo's house, my feet thud down the porch steps while I fume with anger. I have every intention of going home. My car was left at the apartment and it makes me even more mad that I'll need a damn ride.

Across the lawn, Ben and a few others walk along the forest line. I stride to him, making no pains to be quiet about it. Hands in his pockets, he watches me approach warily and his confusion sweeps over me.

"Everything okay?" The people who are standing around him melt away into the trees. He quirks a brow at me. "Kenna?"

"I need a ride home." More anger than I intend seeps through my tone.

"Erm . . . I'd have to ask Evo." He looks up, blinks, and clears his throat. I can hear someone approaching behind me and know it's the man himself.

I poke Ben in the chest. "I don't need *his* say to leave and go home. I'm a free woman and I can do whatever the hell I please. If you don't give me a ride, I have every intention of walking."

Ben puts his hands in his back pockets and averts his gaze, uncomfortable with being poked but keeping his words to himself.

"You're not going anywhere, Kenna. You need to let me explain," Evo speaks behind me.

Recognizing the alpha's command, as Bre had called it earlier when she escorted me into the alpha quarters, I can feel my insides bristle. My wolf, I recognize, is royally pissed and wants me to march right back in and kill the female wolf who dared touch her mate. Perhaps, if there's time, flay Evo alive for daring to command me.

I whirl around so fast that my hair whips my cheek, and poke the alpha standing behind me. "Don't you dare command me to bend to your will. It's not your choice. I want to leave, and there's not a chance in hell you're going to keep me here."

I feel my wolf claw at my insides. She wants to deal with this situation herself and then deal with the female wolf any way she sees fit. It is so tempting. So, so tempting.

Evo's jaw ticks and then he looks at Ben. "Why don't you see if Flint needs a hand running the territory?"

He probably saw my wolf struggling to gain the control and sent Ben off to try to calm me. Or maybe he doesn't want Ben to hear that he was cozying up to another woman just hours after telling me he is my mate, how much he wants me, and how we are 'destined' to be together. Either way, it fuels my wolf's anger even more. She has no plans on keeping secret just how pissed off she is. Neither do I.

Ben retreat into the woods and takes his uncertain emotions with him. "Why don't you go back inside with your *friend*," I growl the last word, "and go seek approval from someone who cares."

This time my wolf growls at me. Actually growls. I can feel the vibrations build inside me and spill out my own mouth. She's angry that I would even suggest her mate go to another's arms.

Hurt splashes over my skin in waves. I scoff to it, feeling a surge inside me rise like a tidal wave.

"Kenna," Evo warns quietly. "You need to reign her in. I can see she's fighting you to shift."

"Check that. I'm not your problem anymore. You don't get to tell me what to do, you don't get to tell me I can't leave, and you sure as hell don't have any ownership of me. You made that very clear when I walked in and witnessed for myself that my own rejection sent you to the first female's arms you came across. I'm going home before I do something I regret. Congratulations. You're free of me and can go right back to that bitch's arms."

I turn and start marching. His hand snaps forward and his fingers wrap around my arm to stop me. That's is all it takes. For the first time, instead of trying to fight her and the rake of claws inside my abdomen, I give in.

It's a punch of adrenaline and fear. A punch through a vail. My body is washed in a wave of consuming pain. Every bone in my body cracks, reshapes, and settles into a new form. It only took a second. Just a split second. One second, I'm eye level with Evo's chest, and the next, he's staring down at me, my clothes in shreds around me. And instead of me being in the forefront of my mind, I am shoved to the back like she always has been. That's when it finally clicks with me – I am a wolf shifter.

A low, deep growl escapes her lips – our lips – directed toward the very stunned man in front of us. Curious about what she'll do, I sit back in my mind and watch like it's a movie.

A moment of hesitation, and he takes a step toward my wolf. She bites the air between us, jaws snapping like a sprung bear trap, letting him know she'll tear him a new ass hole if he gets any closer. She is beyond angry with her mate.

He holds up his hands. "Kenna. Kenna, calm down."

My wolf snarls at him and paws the ground, as if telling him that's not going to happen.

Slowly, he squats to our level. "I'm not a threat." He flashes his wolf eyes at me. "Kenna, you walked in at the wrong time. Listen to me. It's not what you think."

My wolf hesitates, a brief softening, debating if she wants to hear what he has to say next. I couldn't care less. A low growl escapes and vibrates each of my ribs, that's all me. She wants her mate to explain, but I know the truth. I witnessed it. 'Walked in at the wrong time' . . . Ha! I wonder what I would have witnessed if I walked in a few minutes later.

Her ears perk up as we hear a noise from the woods. Two wolves come out from the edge of the trees, their ears high and alert as they begin to prowl their way over to us. I scent the air; *Ben and Bre*.

Evo holds his hand out to the wolves, stopping them in their tracks.

"Kenna, Jazz and I used to be a fling. Nothing more," Evo says to me. I hear Bre growl.

Reminded of the other female touching her mate, my wolf bares her teeth. The snow-white wolf, Bre, recognizes our anger toward Evo. Leaving Ben, a wolf so black he could pass as a shadow in the night, she slowly makes her way over to me. Her head is lowered, showing no threat.

I continue to growl at my mate as he watches, astonished, while Bre's wolf rubs her way along my body, comforting me. Then, she sits at my flank, a show of loyalty. A side picked.

I'm sure Bre heard his words and knew what was going on, especially since she growled when he mentioned Jazz. It's touching that she's siding with me after only just meeting her for the first time.

Evo lets a small smile spread across his face. "I see you've been making friends," he coos. "That's good, baby."

Baby?

My wolf's ears twitch forward and he takes the chance to continue with an explanation, "A show of loyalty such as this," he points to Bre's wolf who's glaring at him with her ears laid back, "shows she supports you as her alpha female, and that she disagrees with her alpha male."

Bre snorts, a puff of air through canine nostrils.

124

"As my sister," he continues through a grin, "she wants to shred me to ribbons. Otherwise, another wolf would never get involved in a disagreement or challenge, especially with mates."

I lean my flank into Bre, letting her know her efforts are appreciated while continuing my death glare at the man in front of me.

He sighs. "Kenna, I'm sorry. Like I said, Jazz and I used to be a fling. But ever since I met you, I've turned her away. It's not easy for a wolf to be turned away. We seek comfort on a regular basis, and she didn't understand my rejection. But now she does because she knows you're my mate. It won't happen again. Please."

Bre and I continue a low and rumbling united front. Hanging his head, his shoulders slouch.

Ben's wolf stiffens as Evo abruptly stands. He pulls off his T-shirt, chucks it to the grass, and starts to strip out of his clothes. Muscle after muscle is revealed to the bright sun, and I perch forward inside my wolf's mind. I study every shift and ripple of muscle as he pushes his pants to his knees. My wolf stops growling as we take in our mate's impressive features. When he removes his underwear, I mentally gulp. *Impressive, indeed.*

His body begins to shake and quiver. Bones twist to take new shape, and golden fur sprouts from head to morphing tail. The color matches his human hair. Confusion sweeps over me. He's shifting but . . . I notice it's taking much longer than it had taken me.

After a few more seconds, a large wolf stands in front of me. Like his human counterpart, he has an impressive build. The wind ruffles the fur along his spine.

Sitting on his haunches, he keeps his head high, and peers down his snout at me. It rubs my wolf the wrong way and she bristles at the show of superiority. We stand there, glaring, statues in the lawn.

The black wolf strides over to acknowledge his alpha and nudges Evo's shoulder in greeting. The movement reminds me of my original anger and my wolf snaps at the males. To her, this is the wolf who let the female touch his human half. He should have torn the female apart. He should have bit her finger off the moment it touched him. He should have –

Evo's wolf huffs at me, stands on all fours, and crosses the last two feet on grass between us . . . as if it is his right to do so. She continues to growl at him, making it clear we want no part in his apology. Even though we felt the *truth* in his words before he shifted, we aren't convinced yet.

Bre leans more into me, a constant support, but he remains unfazed by our prickly attitude. As soon as he's too close, my wolf snarls, lunges, and bites him on the shoulder. Again, he is not fazed, and doesn't even flinch. He stands there, showing no signs of pain as blood dribbles from the minor wound.

He huffs. *Huffs!*

I snarl and lunge for him again, bowling him over. Rolling us, he pins me to my back and lightly snarls a warning in my face – a warning that he doesn't appreciate the aggressive act, and his authority should be recognized.

I snarl back, squirming under his weight. I'm not going to be cowed into submission. My wolf bristles at it and fights to turn the odds in our favor. He isn't getting off that easy for this shit.

We roll through the grass. I land on top of him just as he had been seconds before, and pin him down, growling back in his face.

I can feel more wolves surrounding us, feel their uncertain emotions. They won't involve themselves though. My wolf recognizes this. It's an alpha pair spat. A mate argument.

Something pings deep inside me at this thought. *Alpha pair*. Evo and I, we are their alpha pair, though not mated yet. But since I *am* Evo's mate, that makes me their alpha, too.

My growl fades, replaced with the sound of my heavy breathing propelled by lingering adrenaline. I look at my mate underneath me. Really look at him. He shows no signs of submission. No signs of fear. He's waiting to see what I'll do next, I realize.

Mate, my wolf thinks. The urge to fight evaporates like water splashed on hot pavement.

My wolf's features soften as we come to the same conclusion. My anger is directed at the wrong person. I had felt Evo's truth, and instead of taking my rage out on him, I should be directing at the woman herself.

Pulling herself off Evo's wolf, she sits back on her haunches and gazes around her. The other wolves lower their heads and turn back to the woods, acknowledging that our fight is over. They playfully nip at one another as they disappear into the deep shadows of the trees.

Pack, my wolf thinks, pride puffing her chest.

I watch as Evo's wolf stands up and pads over to me. His movements are graceful and predatory, the wound already clotted. Looking into my eyes for a moment, probably to make sure I won't attack him again, he rubs his muzzle along mine, breathing in deeply as I do the same.

Satisfied that I've calmed, he begins rubbing his entire body along mine, smelling as he goes. A voice sounds in my head, making me jump. *You've accepted me and the pack. We all felt it.* A hesitant pause. *Does this mean you're staying?*

The voice in my head is Evo's, but it scares me enough I begin shifting back to human form, Evo following suit.

Both of us kneel naked in the grass while I stare at him with wild eyes. "Did you – was that – did you just . . . You can communicate telepathically?" I shriek.

He laughs and tentatively kisses my lips, feather-like and gentle. As soft as the kiss is, it sends shivers through my body, heating it to the core. Pleased, my wolf rumbled her content inside me.

The kiss ends sooner than I'd like. "Alpha's can use telepathy to communicate with their wolves," he murmurs. "Mated pairs can also use it."

I frown. "Oh."

His gaze lowers and lingers on parts of my body that make me blush. I try to cover myself with my hands. His smoldering eyes return to mine, and I swear the blue hues within them smolder.

"What?" I whisper self-consciously.

"Do you have any idea how beautiful you are?"

I blink, shocked. No one has ever said those words to me. And the feeling of them – his emotions behind them . . . I know he means it.

When I swallow thickly, he brushes my cheek with his thumb. His calloused finger feels rough against my heated cheeks, and it takes every ounce of my will not to melt into his touch.

He grips my chin softly. "Jazz and I have never had a relationship. We've only used each other to scratch an itch."

I let out a barking laugh. "I guarantee she doesn't see it that way. You don't cuddle with the person you're fuck buddies with."

Dropping his hand, he purses his lips. "I admit, she's shown interest in more, but I've never given her the indication that I was interested. As wolves, we have needs. You can't tell me you've lived your entire adult life not heeding to those needs."

My eyes shift to the space around his head. His jaw ticks at my silent admission. It seems to bother him as much as it bothers me. His jealousy sweeps over my skin and I feel oddly satisfied that the street goes both ways.

"Are you going to hold that against me?" I ask him when the silence stretches on.

He thinks about it for a moment, seeming to choose his words carefully. "No. What happened before I met you was out of my control. You had no idea I was even here, waiting to find you. You didn't even know you were a wolf. I understand the need to find comfort. I had those same needs as well. I can't hold it against you if I also did the same."

"Thank you." Gratitude isn't something that's easy for me to give, so it sounds a little more forced than necessary. "Do you understand how I feel though? To have seen what's-her-twat hanging all over you? *Touching* you? Not an hour or two before that, you were telling me how we are mates; and when I had just come to some kind of understanding of what that meant, I walked in to see *that*."

I didn't want to admit out loud how much it hurt. To have his words sink in and then to witness another female hanging off him like a second skin had been a blow. But it needed to be said.

"Trust isn't easy for you to come by, is it?" When I don't answer, he sighs. "I truly am sorry, Kenna. I'll

130

spend the rest of my life telling you so if it's what you need to hear." When I look down at the grass, he tilts my chin up to meet his eyes. "Do you hear me? You're my mate and I plan to spend the rest of my life showing you that."

I feel his words are true, but the emotion that's still missing is love. I know love is something that has to blossom and grow. It isn't something that happens overnight or I would have been in love at some point during my life. But I'm finding that I am craving it. Continuing to pretend I'd be fine being alone for the rest of my life is pointless. A lie. Everyone wants to be loved. I want to be loved. And I can see myself being in love with him someday.

Cutting me off from my thoughts, Evo asks, "Will you give me a chance? Or do you still want to go back to your apartment?"

I search his eyes and feel his *hopefulness* to have me stay, along with his *fear* that I will leave. It is an all-consuming fear. It makes my heart ache.

I clear my throat. "I'll stay."

A smile spreads across his face. "It's unnerving to hear you so quiet."

He scoops me up, stands, and twirls me around, my naked ass for the world to see.

"Put me down, you asshole. I'm naked!"

He looks down at me, smiles, and then kisses my nose. "There's that prickly attitude. I knew it wouldn't take long." And then, he marches me inside.

CHAPTER EIGHT

Evo Johnson

Relief fills my body when Kenna says she will stay. I was scared she would still want to leave or demand Jazz had to leave.

I know it must be hard for her, knowing Jazz and I have had a sexual relationship, and then to walk in with Jazz trying to seduce me. But still, she didn't ask for Jazz to be banned from the pack and she didn't go marching off to kill her, either. Every wolf has a role to play in a pack, no matter who they are and what they've done. Maybe she knew that and hadn't demanded anything.

I didn't think she was going to shift so soon after finding out what she was. I thought it would take a while for her to accept everything. It came as a surprise that Kenna gave her wolf freedom only hours after learning she's a shifter.

When Kenna shifted, I was sure her wolf would seek out Jazz and rip her to shreds. I've never seen anyone shift so quickly. She shifted in less than a second – that has to be a record or something. She was also wickedly fast – I never saw her bites coming until I felt the pain. It was impressive. *She's* impressive. I suppose this is all normal with being a queen wolf.

No matter, it just adds to her strength as a wolf, a fighter, and a pack leader. It's a strength I wish I had. It's a strength that makes me proud to have her as a mate. And it's hot as hell.

When wolves shift, it's their most vulnerable moment. In a challenge, if they're a slower shifter than their opponent, they would be left wide open, unable to defend themselves while in mid-shift.

If Kenna can shift in a split second, I imagine most of her opponents won't last long. She's fit to be an alpha leader. Born for it. It makes me wonder who her parents were to have abandoned such a gifted shifter child.

I hear the shower turn off and it pulls me from my thoughts. I lift my head to peer at the door and light seeping through the cracks before it opens. Sparing me only a glance, Kenna steps out of the bathroom wrapped in a towel and heads straight for my walk-in closet. Steam follows her like a ghostly tail and water drips from her hair. From the depths of the dark closet, hangers scrape against metal as they get shoved around, then a mumbled, "Fucking hell, none of this will fit me."

I chuckle and sit up in the bed. "Brenna stopped by and dropped off some of her clothes." I grab the bag at the end of the bed and chuck it just outside the closet door. It lands with a soft thud, then skids an inch.

Coming out of my closet with a grateful expression, she snatches them up, adjusts her towel, and then heads to the bathroom to change.

"About this mating thing," I start.

"What about it?" she calls back from the other side of the door.

"There are steps we have to go through and accomplish before the mating is complete." When she doesn't respond, I continue, "It doesn't have to happen in a certain order, or it can happen all at the same time, but there are still hurdles to jump."

She comes out of the bathroom towel drying her hair and sits on my recliner. "I'll bet my last dollar that sex is one of them."

I smile at her crass comment. "Yes, sex is one of them. We have to claim each other in every way possible. Today, you claimed me with your mind. You decided and accepted me as your mate. There are four things that need to be claimed: mind, body, soul, and public."

"Okay, well . . . mind is already done. Body, I'm guessing, is sex —"

Cutting her off, I take over the explanation. "Yes, body would be sex. I plan to explore every inch of

you and fuck every part of you that's fuck-able.
That's something you need to be prepared for." I
watch her throat as she gulps. Her cheeks turn a
shade of pink. "Soul would be our truths, secrets,
fears, things of that nature, to be thrown on the
table for the other see. A mating bond won't be
complete until nothing is left to hold us back from
moving forward. In order to do that, we have to trust
each other with our soul," I pause to take her
frightened expression into consideration. I can tell
that is going to be a difficult one for her. She's lived
on her own for so long and has only had to rely on
herself, trusting no one.

"And 'public' is the claiming mark."

She drops her towel to the floor, an effective
distraction to divert her gaze. "A claiming mark?"

I tuck my chin. "When the time comes, our wolves
will know we're ready to commit to each other for
life. We claim each other by sinking our teeth into
the other's neck, right here." I point to the side of
my neck.

Panic settles in her eyes. Terrified I'll frighten her
off and have her fleeing from the house again, I
quickly reassure her, "Don't be afraid – it won't hurt.
I've been told the bite is so pleasurable, nothing
compares. I've heard some even faint because the
sensation is just too great."

Her fear starts to disappear as my explanation
settles in, and she licks her lips, nervously
sweeping me from head to toe. The smell of her
arousal pumps through the atmosphere and swirls

around me. My wolf rumbles his desire inside me. Holy shit, it smells good. *She* smells good.

I grip the bedding in my hands. Brief flashes of fantasies with my face buried between her legs distract me for a moment. I clear my throat, trying to unclog my thoughts. If we keep up this battle of lust between the two of us, it will keep building until the need to have sex becomes painful. I am already beginning to feel the pain, and as her eyes move below my belly button, my cock twitches, straining against the hem of my jeans.

"Are you okay with all this, Kenna?" My tone comes out deep, laced with desire. "I need to know this is something you are comfortable with."

She shakes her head a little to clear her thoughts. Because of her gift, I'm sure she feels the tension more than I do. "Yeah. Sounds a little loopy, but if you think about it, it makes sense. If there's a person destined to be yours, then there would be stages to go through and overcome. I'm not saying I'm going to be any good at it. I'm a freaking mess on a daily basis." She twists her lips the side and narrows her eyes. I brace myself. "Yes, I'll try . . . on one condition."

I lift an eyebrow. "What's your condition?"

The recline wobbles as she leans forward. "If a female ever touches you again – if you ever *let* another woman touch you again – I'll gut you both like a fish and use your intestines as garland for this year's Christmas tree." With that, she nods once, stands, and adjusts her sweatpants as she returns to the bathroom to brush her teeth.

Her attitude and confidence go straight to my dick. I never thought I'd be attracted to someone so aggressive, *yet* . . .

I adjust my pants. With no relief in sight, I sigh. It can't be normal to be hard all the time. I am starting to worry it'll be stuck – permanently erect for the rest of my life.

A thought crosses my mind, and I blink, wide-eyed, at the bathroom. She doesn't have a toothbrush here.

"Hey!" I shout before dashing to the bathroom. Her playful squeals fill my room.

Makenna Goldwin

That evening, I am introduced to everyone in the pack while sitting at the big table in the alpha's formal dining room. As exhausted as I am, I still notice how supper seems to be a *thing* with these people, and everyone attends like a formal family dinner, minus fancy clothes. At least we're allowed to go in our sweatpants. Not that I would have cared if it was intended to be a formal affair. I still would have worn sweatpants.

I was introduced to the remaining four wolves. The only mated pair in the pack is the red-headed couple, Jeremy and Kelsey.

Kelsey seems to take over the meal responsibilities as her own, claiming she loves to cook when I gape at the artistic display spread across the plates. She's a sweet, but she has a bite to her personality that tells me she takes no crap. I make a mental note to get to know her better. She appears to be happy I'm here, even *feels* happy I'm here, and she kept up most of the conversation as I helped her set the table.

Flint, the charming man with short-cropped hair, and Dyson, the nerdy guy with small glasses, are the remaining two. They joke in the way best friends do, the sort of friendship that revolves around constant insults. Before we even sat down at the table, they had us laughing several times.

I take note that Jazz, who was briefly and awkwardly introduced to me, is sitting at the end of the table. She doesn't look pleased about it. Her anger is thick and directed toward me like little daggers of hate.

With Evo at the head of the table, I sit at the right of him, and Ben sits at his left. Upon observation, we're seated according to rank. I take a little satisfaction in noting Jazz is now at the bottom of the obvious pecking order, whether she decided to sit there out of self-preservation, a pity party, or if she was simply demoted. Either way, the bitch is far from me. I am definitely going to be keeping my eye on her. Though she remains silent but fuming, that doesn't mean she'll be dismissed as a possible threat to me.

"You really never knew you were a wolf?" Flint asks as he chucks a piece of his roast at Bre.

139

It's not the first time I've witnessed Flint's friendly goading of Evo's sister tonight. To Bre's dismay, he continues to give her large amounts of unnecessary attention. It's more than just a friendly vibe he is giving off, too. However, she doesn't return those feelings and scowls at Flint instead of turning into the giggling mess most women descend to when receiving the attention from an attractive male. Any observer would be able to see how much he likes her and how much she finds his child-like behavior annoying. I don't need to be able to feel their emotions to see that tangled web.

I slide a carrot into my mouth and chew slowly. I'm surprised none of the unmated males have mates. They're all extremely attractive. Even the gangling Dyson has this eye-drawing handsomeness about him. I suppose fate has a hand in that and they just haven't met their mates yet.

Jazz, on the other hand . . . a small part of me hopes she'll never meet hers. I can't imagine what her other half would be like. Maybe it would make her a better person. After all, her anger directed toward me has no purpose. Evo is my mate, not hers. He is intended for me. She had to have known this day might come. Did she expect me to walk away from him and hand him over to her? *Not gonna happen, Barbie.*

I startle when I realize they're all staring at me, waiting for the answer to Flint's question.

"No, I didn't," I respond. "I actually thought I was crazy. I had no one there to tell me otherwise, but now that I know, it makes a lot of sense."

"Do you know who your parents are?" Dyson asks, leaning past Flint to peer at me. "I mean, genetically speaking, they have to both be wolves and a mated pair at that. We can't have pups without our mate."

"You'll have to ignore Dyson. He's naturally curious," Evo says as he chews around a hunk of meat. A smile tugs at his lips. I can tell he is enjoying this. He's learning about me without having to ask any questions. I can also feel his joy at the pack's easy acceptance of me, minus one of course. I would guess that accepting a new member to the shifter pack isn't always the smoothest process.

Evo told me earlier – when I had my little fit and attacked him for his wrong-doing – they felt a great deal of respect toward me for the challenging act.

Through telepathy, they had scolded him, and then told him that they respected their alpha female putting their alpha male in his place. Evo said it made them feel more secure – that he wouldn't be able to step a foot out of line without repercussions from me. "A strong alpha pair is what's best for a pack," he had said.

I give Evo a small smile, letting him know I don't mind, which is true. I am going to be a part of their life, something I am growing accustomed to, and frankly, a little excited for. If I am planning to form any sort of friendship with them, it is best they know more about me.

"I don't have any idea who my parents are." I twirl my fork. "I was found abandoned. After they failed

141

to find them, I was placed in the foster system and bounced around for . . . a while."

"Are foster systems as bad as some say they are?" Dyson presses. "There are so many horror stories about them."

Everyone is silent when he asks that question. Evo even stops chewing, wanting to make sure he hears my answer. I can feel their concern, except for Jazz who feels hopeful that I was mistreated and involved in one of these rumored horror stories. It's touching.

"Not entirely." I shrug, pretending to be indifferent. "I went through a lot of foster homes and I never came across someone who stuck kids in dog crates or anything like that. There's just not a lot of love in the foster system. Not the kind you would get from loving parents. At least for me, there wasn't. It really upset me as a kid since I could feel their emotion and could feel that they didn't love me like a real parent would. I know now that I craved it because of my wolf nature, but back then, they thought there was something wrong with me and would ship me out to another home when they couldn't deal with it anymore. I never got put into a foster home that didn't have a bunch of kids in it, so the foster parents never had much time for me, or my problems."

The sound of metal bending permeates the room and all our eyes swivel to Evo. Staring straight ahead with a thunderous expression, Evo's hand holds a bent fork.

Frowning, I touch his arm that's resting on the arm of his chair. "You okay?"

"Don't worry about him," Kelsey says with a roll of her eyes. "Mates don't handle it well when they hear their mate was mistreated. Isn't that right, Jeremy?" She looks at her mate's objecting scowl, and then elbows him in the ribs before he can open his mouth to say otherwise.

I laugh a little as they continue to banter back and forth about overreactions to circumstances of the past. It helps ease the tension in the room that's clogged by Evo's anger and Jazz's juvenile and petty jealousy.

The conversation moves on and we talk about what everyone does for their jobs, a topic I've been curious about myself. It's a relief to hear that shifters are able to work outside the pack. I knew they'd be capable since I've done it all my adult life, but I'm glad it's allowed.

"So, you enjoy being a PI," Kelsey says. It isn't a question, but a statement, since we're now talking about what I do for a living. She dabs her lips with a napkin. "Does your gift help with that?"

The smallest snort comes from Jazz. I spare her a glance, but bite my tongue.

"Sometimes." I pause to sip at my wine. "Sometimes you just don't want to know what others are feeling, and sometimes it's helpful to know what they are feeling. You can learn a lot about someone by how they react to different situations or conversations." I look pointedly at Jazz and everyone snickers. "Emotionally, not everyone can adapt well when the situation calls for it."

Jazz turns from picking at her manicured nails and glares at me. When I don't avert my gaze, she eventually lowers hers in submission. Then, she roughly scoots back her chair and stomps her heeled shoes as she leaves the dining room. Everyone's shoulders drop a fraction when the front door slams closed seconds later.

I turn to Evo and tap the table. "Speaking of investigations, I still need to follow up on Cassie. We need to retrace her steps, maybe see if we can locate where Chris is. I doubt he will leave the state now that he knows the FBI is watching him like a hawk."

"No," Evo says. It is one, very firm, word.

"Excuse me? No?" The table grows silent. They look back and forth between the two of us like a ping pong match, slightly amused.

"Here we go," Kelsey whispers. I hear Jeremy make an oomph sound as Kelsey elbows him in the ribs to drive home her earlier point.

"No, as in you will not be hunting down the murderous, woman-abducting rogue. You're not going to put yourself in danger. I won't allow it."

I pat his shoulder. "You poor thing." Does he honestly think I'll walk away just because things are a bit scary?

"Kenna," he warns, eyes flashing wolf.

I turn to my snickering pack. "Who would like to help me hunt down Kenner before he exposes us to a world full of humans?" I ask in the sweetest voice possible. My mate growls low and dangerous, and it rumbles the table.

Everyone gives wide, slow spreading smiles. I take that to mean two things: one, they're enjoying our spat, and two, I'm positive it won't be difficult to find volunteers.

CHAPTER NINE

Makenna Goldwin

Evo and I banter and bicker about going after Kenner for the rest of the meal, through helping Kelsey with clean up – which she gets a huge kick out of and often chimes in to aid me in my argument – and all the way up the stairs to Evo's room. He doesn't have a choice. Mate or not, he doesn't own me.

In the hallway upstairs, we finally agree that we'll go after Kenner, but I am, in no way, to go after him without Evo.

I don't tell Evo, but I never had any intentions of leaving him behind. I will need help now that I know who I'm dealing with. I decide to keep that to myself and watch him squirm about it instead.

Evo strides in his room, puffed with pride for marginally winning the argument, and holds the door open for me. I don't enter. I stand in the hallway and stare at his bed, then back at him.

Outside, through his open windows, the sky is black and dotted with a pattern of stars. An owl swoops across it, momentarily obscuring the moon.

I gulp. I know if I go into the room, we'll end up having sex. If we lay in the same bed, if we are that intimately close to each other, there's no way we will wake the next morning without having sex at least once before we're up for the day. If we even make it to morning. The question is, is this a can of worms I'm ready to open?

Seeing my hesitation, Evo's eyes search mine. *If you're not comfortable sleeping in the same bed as me, I can sleep in the guest bed down the hall.*

I jump at the telepathy. That is something I am going to have to get used to. I decide to try it out on my own. *I'm afraid,* I admit.

Admitting a fear is not easy for me, but I need to be honest with him. I don't want him feeling like I am rejecting him again because I'm not. There's just so much change happening that I'm having a difficult time adjusting on the spot.

He comes to me and pulls me into his arms, resting his chin on my head and inhaling my scent deep into his lungs. I do the same and greedily drink him in. Inside me, my wolf rumbles with content.

What are you afraid of? he whispers into my mind. *I won't hurt you.*

I'm silent for a few minutes, trying to gather my thoughts to spit out into a sentence. *I'm scared of what it will mean. If we have sex, it will bring us closer. If we have sex, it'll mean something.*

He stiffens. *You don't trust me. You fear I'll hurt you.*

"I don't know you. What am I supposed to think?" I say into his chest. The solid feel of his body and his spicy scent are comforting. Like I'm meant to belong right here, in his arms, forever.

"You're hurt," I add after feeling his emotion.

"I am, but I also understand." His large hand combs through the back of my hair. "I've done nothing to get to know you. I'll have to rectify that. I was supposed to take you to breakfast, remember?"

I smile at the memory. At the time, I was pissed. Now, I find it amusing. Gosh, that memory seems forever ago. Hell, this morning feels forever ago.

He tilts my chin up and pecks my lips softly. His breath fans my face and my eyelids flutter. We pull apart, just an inch, and feel that spark ignite between us. A hungering need fills my lower half when I feel his arousal slam into me with such force. It's a painful arousal, one that's sudden and makes my own body ache. Our breathing becomes quicker and I can't bring myself to pull away from him. The hand on the back of my head suddenly feels sensual and warm.

He steps away, having more strength than I do. Averting his eyes from mine, he whispers, "I'll see you in the morning. Let me know if you need anything."

He walks around me, careful to avoid touching me, and shuts the door softly behind him. The click of the door leaves me a little stunned, and I blink in the darkness.

How could the pull between us be so strong and yet, leave me so weak? He is stronger than me for pulling away, but he was right to. *It is responsible to build a relationship before we complicate it with sex,* I tell myself as I push a hand through my hair.

My knees wobble and it pushes me into action. Distractedly, I make my way to his closet in search of an oversized shirt to sleep in. I'm not even halfway there when the door slams against the wall. I startle and whirl.

Evo stands in the doorway, the light from the hall silhouetting his hulking frame. The smoldering *lust* hits my skin next with such intensity, it sends shocks to my sensitive places. My hands tremble at my sides.

What the hell, I say telepathically, and I then give in to our desires. I rush to him, lips finding his as he meets me halfway. He kicks the door shut behind him and I hop, wrapping my legs around his body in a tight grasp.

Cupping my ass to hold me in place, he walks us to the bed. Our kiss deepens, lips moving frantically, and tongues mingling desperately.

"Kenna," he murmurs against my mouth. "If we go any further, I won't be able to stop. Having sex will further the mating. You can walk away now or . . ." His voice trails off.

I look down at him, chest heaving with adrenaline and desire. For a moment, both of our eyes flash bright green at the same time. "Or you can just cut the shit and get on with it already."

Leaning back a fraction, I lift my top off and fling it into the dark. He growls, a sexy sound, and lowers me to the bed. Rough hands pull my sweatpants off in one swift motion. Then, he stands there, watching me, taking in every inch of my body. I can feel his stare as it touches the swell of my breasts and traces the lace of my underwear.

His brows furrow, but before I prop myself up and can ask him what's wrong, he hooks a finger under my panties, and pulls them down. The bra is removed next and my nipples pebble when they're fully exposed. Every place his fingers touch leaves a hot trail. Goosebumps rise over my skin.

"Holy shit, Kenna," Evo whispers. The moon's beams shine across his face as it seeps through the window, exposing the lust written across his face. He climbs onto the bed, kissing me back into the mattress. "So fucking beautiful."

Wanting more, I begin tugging at the bottom of his shirt, desperate to feel his skin on mine. He notices my struggle, leans back, and removes his shirt. Next, he unbuttons his jeans and pushes them down to the floor.

Before his lips can return to mine, I slide my palms across his chest. I feel every curve and every hard plane of muscle. His skin is so soft and flawless, far smoother than his calloused hands. He moans when my fingers drift down to his underwear and trace the skin along the hem. Using this as a distraction, I forcefully flip him onto his back.

Surprise lights his face, and my bare I s brighten under the moon. A sexy grin rearranges his expression and his lust pulses with more strength, teasing along my skin. I bite my bottom lip and he urges me to continue by rubbing my thighs.

I shimmy past his hips and slide his underwear down, deliberately letting my fingers brush across all his sensitive areas with slow, feather-light touches. A low growl of approval rumbles out of his chest, making a smug smile tug at my kiss-swollen lips. I love how responsive he is.

Feeling something touch my arm, I look down to see his impressive-sized cock flexing and begging for attention. Using the tip of my index finger, I lightly swirl it around his tightened balls, moving at an unhurried pace to the tip and then back down again. Over and over, I repeat this assault until his thighs are quivering. I bend forward and swirl my tongue around the tip, receiving a low and long moan for my efforts. And then, I take him into my mouth.

Unable to control himself, he grabs onto my hair to keep my head in place. My scalp burns to the rough treatment, and I wait, letting him adjust to my torture. He tastes as amazing as he smells, and all around us the world moves on. The hooting owl, the rustle of leaves from the nearby forest, and the tick of a clock somewhere in the house – it all moves on while Evo and I stay stuck in this one moment of him basking in pleasure while I melt into the sensation of his untamed desire.

Breathing heavy, slow, he lifts his head. *Such heat in his eyes.* "You're a wicked little bitch."

I hum my agreement around him, letting the sound vibrate against his length. He hisses and bucks, flexing his hips to fuck my mouth. I dig my nails into his thighs, trying to keep myself steady while he pumps, and pumps, and pumps. The fingers in my hair tug harder, angling my head for his cock to go deeper. Deeper. *Deeper.* The pain heightens my anticipation, and the desperation on his face . . .

Oh, God.

Through watering eyes, I watch him grit his teeth together, feel his legs pick up the quivering, and know he's close to coming. Using my thumb, I search for the soft area just below his balls and apply pressure. His head thumps back to the bed and his chest bows toward the ceiling.

Watching in satisfaction, he yells curses as he comes into the back of my throat, giving me no choice but to swallow.

"Holy shit," he breathes, slumping against the mattress. The bumps and ridges of his abdomen ripple from release. I remove my mouth from his cock and look at him, licking my lips. With his taste in my mouth, I want more. I want release. I want *him.*

Slithering up along his body, letting my nipples graze a path across his stomach, I press my lips to him. They're colder than mine, a bit chapped from panting. He opens, greedily twinging his tongue with my own. I straddle him and lower myself, gently rocking my throbbing clit against his cock that's already hard and ready for more. I moan when I find the right spot, the right rhythm.

"Oh shit," I whisper breathlessly inside his mouth.

He flips me, his mouth quickly finding my nipple while his hand kneads my other breast. "You don't get to pleasure yourself, baby. You're mine. Only I get to make you come."

The flicks of his tongue are desperate and needy, wanting me to be on the same level that I left him. Small sounds of pleasure escape my mouth as he bites down and tugs lightly. Moving to the next nipple, he continues the same while soothing the other's sting with his fingers.

It feels good. So good. I clench the bedding and arch into his mouth. It is like he knows exactly what I want and how my body will respond. The heat of his body against mine, my nipple in his mouth, his breath grazing my flushed skin – it is consuming. Like a blazing fire of pleasure. I've never felt anything like it.

When the sensation becomes too much, I whimper and writhe underneath him. Understanding what I need, he moves lower, kissing his way to my belly button, and then ever lower, until he's settled between my thighs. The sight of him there is nearly my undoing.

153

"Look at me, Kenna." When my heated gaze meets his, he continues, "You're going to watch this. I'm going to eat your pussy, taste you, make you scream, and you're going to watch the whole thing. Anytime you look away or close your eyes, I'll flip you over to spank this nice ass. Understand?"

I gulp. In a raspy voice, I respond, "Controlling fucking bastard."

He plunges a finger in, and I gasp. There was nothing gentle about it, but *holy shit, the pressure feels amazing.* "You're damn right I am. It's mine." He begins to roughly pump his finger in me, applying pressure to all the sensitive places. "All fucking mine, baby. Only I get to make you moan, only I get to make you scream, and only I get to make you come. You're mine, Kenna." His eyes flash bright green.

Knuckles straining, I hold tighter to the bedding, letting out small cries as wave after wave of pleasure consumes me. I'm definitely not going to argue with him on that. If he can make me feel this way, he can have anything he wants.

Slowing his finger fuck, his tongue circles the outside of my pussy, tickling every inch of the bare, sensitive skin. Tracing over and over until I'm quivering with anticipation, he finally flicks my clit with his tongue. His gaze never leaves mine. Not even when my thighs flex around his head.

When he growls at my taste, I let my head fall back – that all-consuming fire takes my breath away. It's almost too much. The swirling finger, the tongue lashing, the heated eyes, the vibration of his growls, my wet and taut nipples. *Oh my God.*

My blazing fire of pleasure stops, a squeak of dismay escapes my lips, and then I'm abruptly flipped face down. A sharp spank to my ass shoots zaps straight to my throbbing clit.

In a split second, I turn to face him, growl, and rake my nails across his chest. Even though the spank was strangely erotic, it's also something my wolf and I have to defend ourselves against. It's an automatic instinct, an alpha instinct, to let our mate know that we won't be cowed into submission.

Evo lowers his head to look at the blood seeping through the scratch, and then lifts his eyes to me. A smile of satisfaction curls his features and I can feel his approval for the mark I gave him.

Leaving the bed, he stands at the end while I continue kneeling and growling at him. Both of our eyes glow, casting the room into green hues. Striking so quickly I almost don't catch the movement, he grabs my thigh and rips it out from under my seat, yanking me to the edge of the bed.

The urge to make this challenging – to challenge him during sex – is strong. It isn't that I think he is going to hurt me. Oh no, this is purely on a primal level. Dominant wolf against dominant wolf. Alpha mate versus alpha mate. It is a need which rides alongside my lustful desires, heightening my sense of purpose toward my own pleasure and our eventual joining.

As he drags me to the edge of the bed, I swing my fist, aiming for his jaw. Evo doesn't anticipate this, and I connect, but it's like hitting a brick wall. His head barely jerks to the side.

He stills his movements and meets my gaze. A hint of humor reaches his eyes. "You better be careful, baby," he whispers softly. "Or I'll skip the fun and fuck you into submission."

My eyes narrow and I'm just about to take another swing when he grabs my wrists and gathers them in one hand. Adrenaline pulses through my veins, a thrill I'm finding addicting. He pins my wrists to my sides and uses his elbows to spread my legs apart. I growl as I try to close them but he's just too strong.

"You fucking cock sucker. You let me –" my voice breaks into a loud moan when I feel his tongue vigorously flicking my clit, swirling and swirling, and flicking and sucking.

"Keep looking at me, Kenna."

"Asshole," I bark.

"Same rules. If you look away, I will slap that sweet ass. This ass is mine. Don't think for a minute I couldn't tell how much you enjoyed it."

This time I have every intention of ignoring his threat. Warningly, he whispers, "Kenna, look at me." Two more times he makes the same demand, and then I am flipped over again. I attempt to scramble to the front of the bed. He yanks me by my ankle at the same time a hand comes down on my ass. A sound between a cry of pain and a moan escapes me. Then, he grabs my hips and pulls them up.

Before I can respond in any way, his tongue penetrates me, fucking me, and all I can do is moan into the bedding. Heat builds in my core like churning lava and the walls of my pussy swell. When he sees that I'm not going to move, he lifts me so my knees are off the bed. His tongue finds my clit, flicking while he slides two sly fingers into both holes. A growl comes from his lips, vibrating around me while he feasts. And that is all it takes.

The heat in my core explodes. I come with a scream and he sticks his tongue back in, tasting me as the white cream rushes to him.

"You taste so good," he says when my shaking subsides. I turn to my back and slowly sit up, pushing the hair from my damp forehead. "So fucking good. I plan to do that again, and again, and again. But right now, I'm going to fuck you and claim what's mine. Are you ready for that, Kenna?"

Horny beyond all belief, sick and tired of the words brimming with promises, I launch from the bed and tackle him to the ground. He grunts as he lands on his back and his hands find my hips as I straddle him. Digging my nails into his chest, I slowly lower myself over his erection.

"Shit," I hiss, wincing against the strain. He's huge. I'm sure it isn't going to fit, but inch by inch and burn by burn, he's finally balls deep inside me. His head rests against the floor and mine falls back. We both groan when the walls of my pussy flutter around him. The stretching, the pain – *the pleasure* – is almost too much. The sensation is ten times what it's ever been.

"So fucking tight," he grunts. His fingers curl into my hips. "More than I ever fucking imagined." He begins to rock me back and forth, rubbing my swollen walls with his dick.

I moan and fist my breast, tweaking my nipples to add to the pleasure. He doesn't like me pleasuring myself, I can feel it. He rears forward, bites my hands away, and takes my nipple in his mouth while continuing to rock me.

When we both moan, he bites down on my nipple. Heat floods through my lower abdomen, spiraling in that familiar way. It keeps building with every rock and touch until it explodes, sending me into a mind-blowing orgasm. My walls clamp down on his cock, forcing him to feel every pulse, tug, and pull.

Evo flips us over and locks his teeth onto my shoulder. Growling possessively, he pounds into me, giving me wave after wave of hot torment. I'm screaming his name, matching him thrust for thrust, desperately trying to form words at how *good* this feels.

He slams into me one last time before he stills. I can feel his come as his explosion rips from him and into me, aiding to the end of my climax. He keeps himself inside me and lightly kisses my slick neck, my flushed cheek, and then my swollen lips, both of us panting and coming down from our orgasms.

"That was, by far, the best sex I've ever had. Nothing about that was normal."

"It's the mating. It'll always be that good." He pulls away from me, meeting my hooded eyes. "I'll never get enough of you, Kenna. If you try to run from me, I'll hunt you down. I'm never letting you go. I meant what I said. You're mine. If I ever find out that another man touches what's mine," flexing his cock inside my pussy helps me understand the part he's claiming, "I'll kill him."

I shove at his chest. "Don't even go there with me. I still want to kill the blonde Barbie bitch for touching you. If I would have found you two having sex, she wouldn't be breathing. Hell, you wouldn't be breathing, either."

CHAPTER TEN

Evo Johnson

The sounds of chirping birds wake me. The most delicious scent swirls around my nose, making my wolf and me content to stay. Pine trees, and damp freshly cut grass, and something else that tugs at my memory.

I open my eyes and find myself protectively formed over Kenna's smaller shape. *Kenna.* Kenna is that 'something else.'

Twice in the night we woke for sex, and countless times over the last few days. I can't get enough of her. She's all-consuming for my mind and body – like she's made for me. She responds so easily and knows my body better than I do.

I'm not the only one whose heart she's won. She's stepped right into pack life as if she's always belonged here. Learning how to patrol the territory with Ben was her least favorite experience, but she had found friendship with Kelsey and Bre, having bonded over their shared love for coffee. And just yesterday, she helped Flint and Dyson change the oil in the pack cars. If their smirks were anything to go by, both were impressed that she knew what she was doing.

Kissing her naked shoulder, I carefully get out of the bed and make my way to my closet to grab my gym clothes. I work out every morning before alpha duties, but now that Kenna has shown up in my life, mornings have been particularly difficult to leave the room. That female is going to be the end of me. *Or maybe she'll be the beginning of me . . .*

I feel warmth in my chest at that thought and turn to stare at her from within the dark confines of the closet. The morning's sun catches the copper mixed in her brown hair, and the sheets are draped around her hips, exposing her slender back to the atmosphere. My wolf rumbles his approval as I slide my sneakers on.

Giving her one last look, I slip out of the bedroom, tread softly down the stairs, and exit through the house's front door. I jump off the porch and land in the dewy grass. My shoes squeak against the wetness as I jog around the front of the house to the back where the pack's gym is.

I could have easily gone out the back door. It would have been faster, but Kelsey is normally cooking breakfast at this hour, and I've been avoiding her questions since the first night Kenna and I had sex. I know it's not details she's after – Kenna wouldn't have hesitated to share those. No, Kelsey is after

161

my side of the story. I just know she wants to know how I *feel* about mating with Kenna.

Women and their damn need to share feelings.

Stepping through the gym door, Ben greets me with a nod, breathing slowly as he curls a heavy weight. Rock music plays across the speakers, not loud enough to drown my thoughts. I stride to the bench next to him and sit heavily.

Out of the whole pack, Ben and I are always the first to rise and generally the last to go to bed, with the exception of whoever's turn it is to run patrol at night. It is our job to make sure the shifters are cared for and protected – to make sure they have everything they need.

When I became alpha, Ben and I saw just how neglected the pack was. No one could physically defend themselves. My father thought it best that the pack didn't learn such things because if there wasn't anyone physically strong enough to challenge him, he would keep his position. That was a mistake and he's lucky it didn't cost him.

If a rival pack ever came in and wanted to take our territory, there would have been no one to defend it and all would have been lost. A pack needs a strong alpha, but the pack doesn't run as a whole unless its wolves are strong, in shape, and mentally sound.

To rectify this, Ben and I make it a priority for the pack to keep up on their physical strength. On weekends, everyone is to work on their fighting techniques, often sparring with other members. It's important they learn to defend themselves and those around them.

Though Ben and I are always the first in the gym, the rest of the pack will trickle in shortly after, usually when they've had the time to consume large amounts of coffee. The sparring will begin after everyone has warmed up.

Ben sets his weights aside and begins wiping them down. When he is finished, he comes over to spot me like he does every morning. I lay back on the bench and curl my fingers tightly around the cold metal bar.

Usually, he uses this time to catch me up to speed on pack business. Today, he takes a different route. "So, uh, did you settle the argument?"

I pause mid-lift and look at him. "We did." *And then some*.

Last night we were arguing about continuing the search for Cassie, the missing girl. We all know she's dead, but Kenna argued that she needs proof for the lady who hired her. Johanna had been calling for updates, and it's eating at Kenna that she doesn't have answers to give her. None she's allowed to give, anyway.

Kenna had spent the last few days interviewing some of Cassie's friends who were at the bar where she disappeared. She hasn't found much that will help with her investigation. My little mate is a feisty kitten when things don't go her way, and she fumed about it last night before I fucked the frustration out of her.

Ben laughs, which is rare for him. He tends to be more on the intense side. "So I heard."

Shifters have very good hearing, but as my beta, his quarters are directly beside mine. I'm sure he heard more than he wanted.

I grunt and then continue my lift. If he's expecting dirty details, he's going to be as disappointed as Kelsey.

"Your mate has quite a mouth on her, doesn't she? I really don't think a single one of us would have gotten away with some of the names she called you."

That brings a smile to my face. Kenna called me every name in the book last night. Some were completely made up. I loved every minute of it. She battles me for dominance – through sex or everyday conversations. Whether she realizes she's doing it or not, it's completely arousing.

She's exactly what I need and everything I didn't know I ever wanted. I'm making it a point to spend as much time with her as I can. I want to get to know her, and let her get to know me. I want the mating completed as quickly as possible. I want her to be completely mine in every way. So, I've been rectifying that by taking her on dates. Walks mostly, but I've taken her to lunch twice.

"The pack loves her," I say, a slight change in subject. Aside from Jazz who has made herself scarce, everyone often migrates to her without realizing they are doing it. I think if she would allow it, any one of them would be happy to give her foot

164

rubs and hand-feed her skinned grapes every night. She won't stand for that sort of pampering, though. She'd outright object to the idea of such a thing. I smile again at the thought of my prickly mate.

"Has Jazz tried to gain your attention again?" Ben asks.

"No. She's avoiding both Kenna and me, thankfully. Has she come to you for anything?"

"Not really. She asked to borrow one of the pack cars a few times to go out to the bars, but that's about it. She's avoided any topic about you or Kenna."

"Have you tried talking to her about it?" Ben's job as beta is to be there for anyone who has concerns. As much as I'm glad Jazz is listening and staying away, I don't want one of my wolves to be at a loss. Even if that loss is me. If she's hurting, I want her to be able to go to someone. She doesn't have a lot of friends here. She's more or less tolerated. The pack had gotten along okay with her, but ever since they found out she tried to cozy up with someone else's mate, alpha's aside, they've been noticeably indifferent toward her. It's understandable, but rejection has to hurt on some level.

Ben sighs. "Yes. She swears she's fine."

"I suppose we'll have to take her word for it then."

Flint walks in, waves groggily, and heads straight for the treadmill to warm up. Getting the machine started, he looks at me as he settles into a jog.

165

"Kenna learn anything new yesterday during the interview?" he asks.

Setting the bar back on the ledge, I sit up. Ben chucks a towel at me and I pat my brow with it. "No. Everyone is saying the same thing that Cassie's friend, Jackie, said."

"We may have to make a field trip to the bars then. See if anyone has seen that guy. You have a picture, don't you?" Flint asks.

I nod. "That sounds like a good idea. I'm afraid there isn't much of a choice but to go hunt him down and see if he's crawled out of the hole he's been hiding in."

Kenner had disappeared off the radar since the questioning. He hasn't used his passport, hasn't flown anywhere, hasn't used any credit cards. He knows he's being watched and now he's laying low.

"There's no way he left the area. It wouldn't be smart for him to relocate. Not when everyone's eyes are trained on him," Ben speaks from behind me.

Flint pretends not to hear what Ben says. "I bet he's still in the area," he speaks directly to me. I can hear a sigh escape Ben from behind me.

Knowing what is going on between them, I won't get involved. I hope they figure it out soon before it turns into something more. Then I *will* have to get involved.

All I know is that it revolves around my sister. Flint likes Brenna, Brenna likes Ben, and Ben likes being beta. Flint sees Ben as a potential rival for Brenna's affections. What Flint doesn't see is that Ben is showing no interest in Brenna. If he did, he's hiding it carefully. I have every faith that the three of them will figure it out eventually. Personal business isn't my business unless it involves the pack, and this, fortunately, is not pack business. Not unless it grows out of control to the point where even the beta can't tame it.

"You're both right. We'll head to the bars tonight." I look at Ben. "You'll be staying behind with Jeremy and Kelsey. I'm positive they won't have any interest in going to the bar and we need people here to watch the territory. I want you three to run the perimeter until we get back. I don't want any surprises."

Ben nods as I get up and go to a treadmill, and as Jeremy comes through the door, Ben meets him half and begins explaining tonight's plan.

Makenna Goldwin

It's mid-morning, and I am slightly annoyed that I woke up in the bed alone. Seriously, what time does this guy normally wake up?

Taking my mug of coffee from the kitchen's massive island, I head into the dining room and open the sliding back door which leads to the porch.

Since I've been here, Kelsey has been making my coffee every morning, and every morning I sip from my dark brew on the back porch and plan out my day. Today, I need to decide what I intend to do to further my investigation. I seem to be going nowhere talking to the friends, but I have one left that I plan to meet with. To do that, I need to leave the territory. That involves a game plan.

As soon as I pull the sliding door open, I hear chatter, laughter, and several "oofs." Curious, I step outside, bare feet settling on smooth wood.

All the wolves, minus Ben and Evo, are sparring. I frown and grab the back of a porch chair. As I drag it over to sit and watch the scene unfold, Bre climbs the porch steps to greet me. I grab another chair and settle it next to mine.

Cheeks flushed and skin sweaty, she sits down at the same time I do. I ask the obvious question, "Is this normal to beat the shit out of each other on a Saturday morning?"

She laughs and props her feet on the wooden rail. "Yep," she says, popping the 'p.' "Evo likes to keep us fit in case we get jumped."

"Sure, sure." I nod and sip gingerly from my mug. "So why aren't you out there getting in on the action, then?"

She gives me a pointed look. "Because my sparring partner is still guzzling her go-go juice."

"You and me? Sparring?" I never really had the chance to spar with another person when I was at the apartment's gym. Believe it or not, not a lot of people do that anymore. Less than half the apartment complex actually blessed their bodies with physical activities and a little sweat.

"Yep," she says, popping the 'p' again.

Grabbing my mug, she takes a sip of my coffee. She closes her eyes and sighs. "Strong and bitter, just the way I like it." She then hands the mug back to me.

A normal person might find it offensive if someone did that – stole their drink for a swig – but I don't. I'm at ease here. I feel accepted and everything I do seems acceptable, almost as if I've known these guys my whole life.

Comfort isn't hard to reach, as the pack seems to touch me whenever they float by with a gentle back rub or a shoulder squeeze. It's serene and soothing, which is something I've never had and never experienced. I'm coming to care for this pack and everyone in it. *Minus one.*

Looking up, I see Kelsey and Jazz circling one another. They aren't so evenly matched, but I note that Jazz seems to fight dirty, often using her nails instead of knuckles. Dodging and weaving, Kelsey narrowly avoids them.

Bre and I watch as Jazz takes another swipe at Kelsey, leaving a thin trail of blood on her cheek. Kelsey's eyes glow wolf and she swings, closed-fisted, at Jazz, landing a punch square on her nose.

I wince but Bre chuckles. "Never go for Kelsey's face," she advises in a murmur.

"Noted."

"How'd the move go? Did you get everything you needed?"

Yesterday, after a few interviews with some of Cassie's friends, I decided it wasn't worth keeping my apartment. Seeing and feeling the sorrow her friends felt for their missing friend had sparked something in me. I didn't want to miss another minute with my pack mates and I sure as hell didn't want to miss another minute with Evo.

It was a big surprise to Evo when I pulled up in his SUV with all my belongings jammed inside. I could feel his excitement that I made the move-in official and was taking the next step without any prompting. He was overjoyed that I accepted the pack's home as my own and planned to stay. His joy turned smug when I told him I sold my car.

I knew I wouldn't need my rusted hunk of junk here. The pack has several cars available to use and they're more dependable, too. It was still despairing to hand the key over to that pimple-faced teenage kid, though. I know Hunk won't last long under that kid's care.

"It did." I nibble on my lip. "Hey, thanks for letting me borrow your clothes before. All of Evo's stuff is massive. I appreciate it. I'm gonna have to borrow the black top again, though."

Bre lifts an eyebrow. "The sleeveless sequin one?"

"Yeah." I nod and take a sip. "It's totally sexy. I wore it on our date the other night."

"Sure thing. You can wear it tonight when we go out to the bar. There's a black sequined skirt that goes with it. It makes it look like a short black dress. You'll borrow that, too."

I blink. "We're going to the bar tonight?"

"I overheard Flint and Dyson discussing it."

We watch as Kelsey plows Jazz over, and this time we both wince as Jazz spins and hits the ground hard. Kelsey is a beast. I love that girl. Not only is she an amazing cook, but she is quick-witted *and* ruthless.

In my peripheral vision, I see Bre's eyes move to Ben and a *longing* drifts over my skin. Staggered, I jerk in my seat and blurt, "You love him."

Startled by my outburst, she gawks at me. "What? Who?"

I huff and lower my voice. "Don't you start with me. Anyone who's paying the least bit attention can see that you have a thing for Ben. I just happen to be able to feel it."

Her shoulders sag as I take another smug sip of my coffee. "I keep forgetting about your gift. You don't flaunt it like most would expect and that's appreciated. I thought it would be unnerving to have someone around who can feel what I'm feeling, or if I'm being dishonest, and then dangle it out in the open. It takes a loyal person to keep that to yourself."

"You're avoiding the subject," I sing-song, twirling a finger in the air.

I'm touched by what she confessed. I never thought of it that way. I only thought that it was none of my business. Never would I betray someone I care for by hanging their dirty laundry.

She snatches my mug back, takes a sip, and talks into the mug as I tap a nail on my chair's arm, "Yes, okay? Yes, I love him."

I snatch my mug back, gulping this time.

"He's my mate."

I choke on my coffee as it slides down the wrong pipe, flabbergasted by her admission. "Excuse me?"

"Ben is my mate."

"No, I heard that. It's just . . ." I trail off as I glance around. "Look, I felt the pull to Evo, and I didn't even know what he was to me at the time. The pull is so primal it's almost painful."

She sighs, looking at Ben again. "I know."

Setting my mug down on the rail, I stand up and stretch. "Does he know? That you guys are mates, I mean?"

She stands up with me, briefly stretching. "I don't know," she says. I follow her down the steps and to an empty space in the lawn. It's private enough for us to continue our conversation.

We get into our fighting positions. "If he does, he doesn't show it. Either he's so consumed with beta work that he can't feel the mating or," she swings at me, but I am prepared and easily dodge, "he's acting like I don't exist because he has no interest in mating. He takes the beta role pretty seriously."

I land a jab to her ribs and hear her lungs gush out air. She bends, grasping her side. "Damn it, Kenna, you're fast." She rights herself and gets back into position.

"Do you want me to kick his ass?" I ask while she attempts a series of strikes. I manage to dodge every one, except for a blow to the arm which makes my hand go numb.

"What?"

Shaking my hand to get back feeling, I give her my best solution. "I can totally kick his ass. Make him see the light and all that."

She smiles at the thought. "Tempting, but I want my mate to come to me because he wants me, not because our badass alpha queen spanked his ass and set him straight."

I laugh as I abruptly squat to the ground and stick out a leg. I turn and trip her, and she falls flat on her back with a grunt.

Scrambling over, I quickly straddle her. "What about Flint?"

I aim to land a series of punches, but she rolls us until I'm flat on my back. A blow to my ribs and I hiss at the pain. Then, I use my leg to flip her to the ground.

When both of us jump up at the same time, she replies, "What do you mean?"

I land a hit to her chin and she curses. Blood instantly oozes from the corner of her mouth and she wipes it away.

"He's got a thing for you."

Her eyes flick to Flint. He's sparring with Jeremy and Dyson. It gives me the opportunity to jab her hip.

"Fucking hell, Kenna." Stumbling back, she rubs her hip. "Do you have any idea how fast you move?"

I give her an apologetic smile and let her recover. When she places weight back on her leg, we continue.

"He stares at you all the time. Haven't you noticed?"

She throws several punches, each blocked as I discover her fighting techniques and strategies. "I've noticed a lot of food in my hair."

Flint had continued his version of flirting each evening meal like a five-year-old with a school-girl crush. Even I am growing tired of it. Now that I know Bre and Ben are mates, I understand the cold shoulder Flint directs at Ben. Maybe Flint doesn't know Ben and Bre are mates, but he sure isn't paying attention to the fact that Ben's attention isn't on Bre.

"But no, I haven't noticed. Once you know who your mate is, all the other males sort of . . . I don't know . . . drift from your thoughts. You see them, but they don't hold interest to you."

I can understand that. I notice how attractive the Cloven Pack males are but feel no sexual attraction to them. It's merely an observation. It's nothing compared to looking at Evo.

We don't talk for a while, each trying to gain the upper hand and getting lost in our own thoughts. We're closely matched, but I still manage to connect and dodge more than she does. I suppose that comes with being alpha. The strongest and fastest lead the pack. But still, Bre is well-versed in fighting techniques. I'd hate to be Ben if she ever got pissed enough at him for ignoring her and their mating.

Panting with exertion, we both bend over, resting our hands on our knees as we look at each other.

"Is it normal to be that fast?" I hear Dyson whisper. Turning our heads, we see that his whispered question is directed at Evo. We had gained the audience of the entire pack who had circled around us during our practice.

"It is if you're a queen," Evo rumbles with his arms crossed. He gazes at me, his eyes half-hooded. I don't need to feel his emotions to know what that look means – something I've done has turned him on.

"This girl has some serious moves, Evo," Bre says between pants as she stands up fully. "Next time, you spar with her. It'll be more evenly matched."

He grunts as he continues to look at me. I wipe blood off my cheek and feel the pack melt away. All are chatting away about a new move they learned or who won which match as they enter Evo's quarters.

Gathering in his living room is a normal occurrence for my pack. It's natural to want to be in the presence and comfort of the alpha pair, even if that means constantly invading their living room or snack cupboard. Since I've been here, Kelsey and I have had to go to the store twice already, just to restock.

"It's hard to believe you let a new vampire get the best of you," Evo rumbles.

I frown and stand fully upright. "I have a perfectly good excuse for that. He was a freak show and it was slightly distracting."

"M-hmm." I gulp as his lust slams into me. "Do you have any idea how hot you look right now?" he says as the sliding door shuts.

He starts to walk toward me, stalking his prey, and I back up until my spine hits a tree.

Reaching for me, his lips land on mine, devouring, demanding, and taking, while a hand cups my sweaty cheek. His hand then moved to grab the back of my hair and he pulls my head back for a deeper kiss, pinning me to the tree with a press of his hips. My body responds easily to his, and before I know it, my pants are gone and he's untying his own.

I pull my mouth away and glance at the porch's sliding door. "Wait, Evo. They'll see us. Let's go –"

"They won't watch, Kenna. If they know what's good for them, they won't dare."

He begins kissing my neck and I take the moment to gaze around, still unsure. Sure enough, we're completely alone. The birds chirp in the branches above us, and a bunny hops across the grass, but otherwise . . .

Evo tugs on my hair. "Relax, baby. No one will watch." I bite on my bottom lip and he captures my mouth. Grabbing my ass, he lifts me up, angles my hips, and slams his dick into me. I grip the bark above my head and groan to the sky. Evo whispers curses and rests his forehead against my sternum.

A breeze swirls around us, urging us on, and he pounds into me. His rhythm is merciless, desperate, and his desire is delicious. I let Evo consume me, let my name from his lips seep into my heart.

My mate bites at my breast through my shirt. Goosebumps flare across my skin at the same time a wave of heat soars through my veins. He slams over and over again, the bark of the tree biting into my spine.

I'm so close. So close to exploding around him.

"Evo," I whimper. Bark breaks away and crumbles in my grip.

"You like that, Kenna? Do you want more, baby?" At my whimpering answer, he reaches between us and pinches my clit. The pumping of his hips makes his hand rock just enough to – to –

"Come for me, baby."

And that's all it takes. I arch into Evo and scream as I come, my pussy milking Evo's cock as we reach our climax together.

"Shit!" he hisses. He kisses me, desperate at first, until our climax ends and the pumping dwindles to nothing. Using his body to keep me against the tree, his kiss turns into something more sensual and loving. Something that speaks more than words could ever.

That's when I feel warmth directed toward me from Evo. It's a feeling I can't describe, but such a wondrous feeling to feel. There's this aching void in my chest I didn't know was there, and now, it's being filled.

"You love me?" I whisper, guessing at the emotion he's giving off.

His expression gives nothing away. He pulls back and slides out of me. Gently, he sets my feet on the ground and helps me pull my pants back on before grabbing his own.

"I do," he finally admits. My heart floods with relief. The hole begins sealing itself up, containing what filled it.

I reach up to his face, running my hands through his hair. "Is this what it feels like to be loved? To feel so . . . whole? To feel put back together when you didn't know you were in pieces?"

"It must be," he says, brushing his lips against my eyebrow.

"You've never been in love before?"

He shrugs. "I've known love. I love my sister. But I don't know love past that point. I never knew my mother; she died during childbirth with Brenna and I was too young to remember her, so I don't know that kind of love, either." He straightens the wrinkles from my shirt. "Anyone I've had a fling with was just that and nothing more. I've never been in love before. This is new to me, too."

My heart breaks for the loss of his mother. I can appreciate that pain. I never knew my parents. Understanding pack life a little better, there had to be a reason for them to abandon me. There had to be more to that story.

Packs, at least the Cloven Pack, seem to be close knit. If my parents didn't want me, then surely someone else in their pack would have taken me in. Or maybe that was the reason. Maybe they were keeping me from the pack or saving me from it. Hearing about Evo's father being a cruel alpha, maybe that's why they abandoned me . . . to keep me safe.

It is a comforting thought that maybe I wasn't abandoned because I wasn't wanted. It's a small sliver of hope I can hold onto. Maybe someday, we will be reunited and they can explain.

There are a lot of unanswered questions and none I have any means of discovering. Now that I know what I am, the idea of finding them is more intriguing. I want to learn more.

"What about your dad?" I place my hand on his chest and feel the steady beat of his heart. "How did he survive the death of his mate?"

Flicking a ladybug off his pants, he replies, "I've been told my mother was a very kind soul, generous down to her bones. My dad has always had a dark side. When mates are brought together, they fit like a puzzle piece. Each piece of yourself that you give the other creates a picture. It alters them to their very core, and together, you become one. It can create a beautiful picture, a terrifying one, or sometimes, the puzzle lay unfinished."

Losing himself in thought and memory, he pauses for a moment. "My mother was too generous and my father too greedy. They were so stuck in their own ways that they rebelled against each other. They loved each other, but they wouldn't give into the mating completely. They wouldn't let each other share pieces of themselves in fear they would become something other than who they were. Each of those characteristics – generosity and greed – ruled their lives. It ruled their lives so much so that the mating wasn't a strong one, but a forced one. When that happens, a mate can survive the other's death. It is rare, but that's what we believed to have happened."

I nod. That makes sense. If you fight the mating – the shaping of your life to fit that of who you belong to – your relationship won't be a strong one. Like Evo said, if a mating is like a puzzle and you try to force certain pieces of that puzzle together, the puzzle won't hold.

 "I'm sorry, Evo." And I am. I know it isn't my fault and I had nothing to do with how he grew up, but my heart still aches for him. He deserved better.

He tucks a stray hair behind my ear. The gesture feels like gratitude. "Come on, baby. Ben needs to meet with me."

CHAPTER ELEVEN

Evo Johnson

Ben takes a seat across from my desk as I lean back in my office chair. He brought a folder with him and I'm curious as to what it contains.

"I looked into Chris Kenner's history," he begins.

His cryptic words make me raise my eyebrows. Patience isn't always my strong suit.

"Go on," I wave.

"He's from the Gray Pack."

I frown. "I don't recognize the name of that pack."

"I didn't either, so I did some digging." He drops the folder on the desk. "Their territory isn't far from here. About fifty miles. The alpha is extremely . . . difficult. He runs his pack like a cult. He basically makes his shifters worship him and he never lets them leave their territory. From what I hear, he's controlling and very much on the loony side."

I pick up a pencil and tap it against the desk. "So, what does this have to do with Kenner? How did he get banned?"

Ben clears his throat. "He didn't. Kenner is the Gray Pack alpha's son. He ran a few years ago because he wanted to find his mate. Since his father wouldn't let his wolves off the territory, he did the only thing he could. He left while his father was unaware. The alpha is still looking for him today."

"So, going rogue is what turned Kenner insane. He couldn't join another pack because his father would find out." I point the pencil at the unopened folder. "I'm also guessing he never found his mate."

"That's what I'm thinking, too. It's rough to hold onto sanity when you're not a part of a pack. Lord knows how Kenna did it. Did you notice his victims are always female?"

"Yeah, I did, but I couldn't find any other connection besides that."

"I have a theory." Ben slouches, spreading his knees wide as he relaxes into his chair. "If his wolf went insane, doesn't it make sense that his wolf was searching for his mate, trying to find her in any female he showed interest in, then lead that female to her death when his wolf discovered she wasn't his mate?" Ben has always been excellent at reading people and discovering what makes them tick. It's what made him the obvious choice for beta.

"Hmm. That's a good theory. I wonder why he hasn't taken anyone recently."

Ben shrugs. "Your guess is as good as mine. I have the pack alpha's number here if you want to give him a call. It might be a good idea to let him know we are going after his son."

I consider this, eyeing the folder as if it'll shout all the answers to my questions. We probably should let the alpha know, even though I'm not looking forward to having a conversation with this guy. If the situation were reversed, I would want to be informed on one of my missing wolves.

I nod and grab my phone from my pocket, dialing the alpha's number as Ben rattles it off from memory alone. "His name is George Kenner."

I nod and listen to the phone ringing. "Hello?" a female voice answers.

"Hello, this is Evo Johnson, Alpha of the Cloven Pack. Who am I speaking with?"

"Oh, ah . . ." A rude smacking of what I can only guess is bubble gum. "This is Victoria. Um – I'm not – I'm just a member of the pack I mean, I don't have any authority. Do you want me to get my alpha?"

I raise my eyebrows. This female wolf is extremely nervous. "Yes, that would be wise, Victoria."

I hear her set down the phone without another word. In a minute or two, the phone is picked up and a gruff voice comes through the receiver. "This is George. Who's calling?"

"Mr. Kenner, this is Evo Johnson, Alpha of the Cloven Pack."

"What do you want?" he growls. His voice is raspy, as if he smokes cigars on an hourly basis.

I frown. Not only does he run the pack like a cult, he is a rude fucker. "I'm calling about your son, Chris."

"I haven't seen Chris in years. Whatever he's done to you and your pack is no business of mine. What's this about?"

I sigh, already sick of this conversation. "We believe he's gone rogue and is running loose in our city. We have reason to think he's abducting and killing women."

The receiver is silent for a few seconds. "He's here? I'll take care of this. Is that all?"

"Actually, George," I am done with trying to show this guy any ounce of respect, "this is now my responsibility. He's tried attacking one of my wolves already, aside from recklessly rampaging through this town and chancing the discovery of wolf shifters. The FBI is already on him and they're keeping a close watch. I don't plan to hand him over to you, nor do I plan to let him live."

I am well within my right to take care of this situation. If another wolf goes after another pack, it is within that pack's right to deliver justice. There is

185

no way I am going to tell him Chris went after my mate as well because that would mean that I, myself, have every right to kill him. Something tells me that information would tip George over the edge.

"You will do no such thing," George barks into the receiver.

"Oh, I will." I twirl the pencil between my fingers. "This is not your problem anymore. Chris has gone rogue and there's no saving him. He attacked a member of my pack, and we are within our right for retaliation and justice. We will deal with him as we see fit."

"You will –"

"I called to keep you informed on a wolf who you let go rogue. I don't care if he's your son."

"You'll regret this! If you kill him, you'll regret this. My wolves and I will come after you!"

"Then, I suppose we'll be waiting for your visit. Have a good day, George." I hang up the phone.

Ben, who has an amused expression, heard every word with his wolf hearing. "That was . . . interesting. Think he'll live up to his word?"

"I have no doubt." I flare my nostrils. It's been a while since I saw any action. A part of me is hoping he does retaliate. I can be ruthless if I need to be, and my pack is more than ready for such a challenge. It's what I've been preparing them for.

"I'm looking forward to it. Should I be planning for such a thing?" Ben smiles, toothy and predatorial.

"Probably. Let's table that for now. What else you got?" I incline my head to the folder on my desk.

Ben looks at me sheepishly. "Uh . . . well . . . I wanted to wait until you made that call before I told you the rest. I figured it would cloud your judgment."

"Oh?" I lean back in my chair and press the pencil's eraser to my cheekbone.

"While I was looking up Kenner's information, I also found a few things about a missing child who was reported by a – er – pack."

"Ben, if you don't get on with it, I will seriously punch you in the face. After dealing with that asshole, I'm in no mood. Use your words. Explain what the hell you're talking about."

Ben flips opens the folder.

I read about the child. Brown hair and brown eyes, whose date reported missing is the day before Kenna was found. My heart sinks.

"Which pack is she from?"

Makenna Goldwin

In the alpha's living room and on the plush couch, Bre is laying her head on my lap while the entire pack, minus Ben, Evo, and Jazz, are peppered on the remaining furniture. The TV mounted on the wall is softly playing a documentary that's lulling me to sleep.

How odd, I think to myself, yawning. If someone would have told me a few weeks ago I'd be living with a man I love, discovered I had a wolf heritage, belonged to this family we call a pack, *and* be attacked by a vampire hired by a psychotic wolf shifter who's lost his marbles, I would have laughed in their face. So much has changed. *I have changed.* Before, I didn't know it was possible for someone to change on such a fundamental level to where the world no longer feels like the world I grew up in. I never actually believed people could change, yet, here I am, stroking Brenna's short hair in the comfort of the place I now call home.

Bre's shoulders shake as she laughs at something Flint said. It pulls me from my sleepy thoughts.

"Remember that time when you first started working out?" Flint asks Dyson, already snickering at the memory. He sits on the chair swiveled to face us and rests his elbows on his knees.

"Don't you say it, man!" Dyson threatens from the other chair. He jabs a finger in Flint's direction.

Smiling and curious, I look at Flint. "Do tell."

Flint licks his lips. "Well you see, Dyson thought he was a badass and . . . Son of a bitch!" Flint yells. Dyson had thrown his shoe at him and it hit him square in the jaw. He cups the side of his cheek, gawking at his best friend. We all laugh at the dramatics.

"He decided it would be a grand idea to read while running on the treadmill," Flint presses on, his gaze promising revenge. "When he was done running, he shut off the machine, stepped off, and fell flat on his face!" Flint dramatically demonstrates with both hands.

Defending himself, Dyson shouts over our noise, "Oh, come on! It was a case of vertigo! You can't tell me that it's never happened to any of you before!"

From the other couch, Kelsey and Jeremy roar with laughter, and Kelsey replies, "Well, of course not! None of us have tried to squeeze in a chapter during a two-mile run!"

"Must have been a damn good book." I chuckle.

"It was important," he replies, a sheepish blush overtaking the natural pallor of his cheeks. "The newest addition of advanced programming. It had just arrived in the mail!"

"That's even worse, Dyson," Bre replies.

My stomach hurts and tears are streaming down my face from laughing so hard. While Dyson pretends to be offended at us finding his predicament hilarious, I know his feelings aren't hurt. I feel amusement coming from him. He's enjoying being a part of a joke.

Thundering steps come from the stairs and Ben and Evo round into the living room. Immediately, I know Evo is trying to hide something. The vibe he gives off feels like oily secrets, and by the set of his jaw, he's upset. Ben . . . well, Ben is straight up angry with red splotchy cheeks and his eyebrows knitted together.

I frown and straighten my spine. I'm just about to ask what's going on when Evo looks at me and shakes his head slightly, letting me know through telepathy that we'll discuss it later.

Evo rolls his shoulders and addresses the pack as a whole. "We're going to leave tonight and head to the bar where Kenna's witness last saw Kenner. Hopefully we can find a lead on him."

Jeremy stands and stretches. "Did you learn anything new?"

"You're supposed to be on patrol," Evo says to Jeremy, squinting his eyes in accusation. Jeremy pockets his hands and tucks his chin.

"We found out a little about him," Ben interrupts. "We're hoping we can use the information to our advantage."

Everyone is silent as he makes his way around the couch. He scoots Bre over to the other side and sits between us. Roughly, he scrubs at his face.

"He's from the Gray Pack," Evo mutters. At everyone's frowns, he holds up his hand to stop the questions from spilling out of our mouths. "It's a very secluded pack. He wasn't banished. He had left on his own when he decided to search for his mate. I already talked to their alpha and he's not happy that we plan to deal with this on our own."

"Why?" I bark.

Ben drops his hands and answers, "Chris Kenner is the alpha's son."

Silence settles across the room and Evo's the one to break it. He reaches for the remote on the couch's arm and shuts the TV off. "We need to be prepared since the Gray Pack may come knocking on our door."

"Should we call for backup?" Flint asks.

Evo returns the remote to the couches arm, gently setting it down and straightening with an unsettling calm. "Ben thinks it's a good idea to see if the Riva Pack would be willing to stand beside us if it comes down to it. Do you still have your connections to that pack?" he asks Flint. Flint nods. "Good. Why don't you put in a call and have their alpha call me when he's available."

"The Riva Pack?" I ask.

"They're friends of ours," Bre supplies quietly. "A neighboring pack. Some of our old wolves transferred there."

As I pull my hair back and wrap a ponytail around it, I sort the many emotions slithering across my skin. Worry, mostly, but I can tell Evo is leaving information out. I resolve to ask him more details later. It's important that I know everything for my investigation.

Evo looks at me. "Kenna, baby –"

"Hmm?"

He crosses his arms loosely. "Ben and I discussed it. We think it best if you stay behind." I start to object, but he doesn't let me get a word in. "I know this is your fight, but if we run across Kenner, he'll have a harder time recognizing one of us instead of both. If he catches sight of both of us, he will run before we ever get the chance to catch him." That isn't the only reason, I can tell. It is just a half truth, but I can't focus on that. I can only focus on the fumes bubble in my chest.

This is *my* investigation and finding Cassie's abductor is *my* responsibility. I'm also mad because I know he has a point. The fewer recognizable people, the better.

Taking the opportunity of my silence, he continues, "I'll take Ben in your place and you'll stay with Kelsey and Jeremy." I blink in question. "They're staying behind because we can't leave the territory undefended." Evo tips his attention back to Jeremy and gives him a pointed look. Without hesitation, Jeremy weaves between the furniture and exits out the front door.

"It would be irresponsible if we allowed someone who isn't familiar with shifters to take on a rogue," Ben whispers.

Averting my gaze to the black TV screen, I mumble some not so nice things under my breath, and cross my arms over my chest. I'm so angry that I don't even want to look at them.

"I'm going to stay behind, too," Bre announces. Shocked, I peer past Ben's shoulders. She turns to me and smiles sheepishly. "I'll keep you company."

I know why she isn't going. With Ben part of the group who's going to track Kenner, and the lustful atmosphere of a bar, it would be a blow to her. Nothing would suck more than watching the man you love being approached by other women, nor watching other couples have what you don't have. And then to have Flint there as well. He would definitely be laying on the moves. I've gathered that the 'ladies' are his hobby. Avoiding all of that would be a less stressful night, and staying here is what's emotionally best for her.

I can feel her relief when Evo nods. Eventually, I'm going to have to do something with this Ben and Bre thing. Seeing her hurt like this, and trying so hard to hide it, breaks my heart. I've come to love my mate's sister, and Ben is getting close to landing on my shit list for ignoring her. I can feel that he doesn't see her as anything but another shifter to care for, which means one thing: he's completely oblivious that his mate is to his left. I clench my jaw and peer at the side of Ben's tired face. It's making me question if he's even interested in finding his mate.

"So, what do we do when we see him?" Flint asks, rubbing a hand over his short hair. Though his question is directed at Evo, his eyes are searching Bre's face, trying to find the real answers to why she's staying behind. I'm going to have to do something about the Flint and Bre thing, too. I sigh. I'll just add that to my to-do list. I sort of feel bad for Flint. If Ben and Bre ever do get together, I may have to help him through it if he doesn't come to terms on his own.

Evo spares me a glance at the sound of my annoyance. He's probably assuming I'm throwing a tantrum about not going. Though I'm annoyed with being left behind, I'm more concerned with the love triangle that is plaguing my pack at the moment. A triangle of doom.

"I don't want anyone roaming around by themselves," he eventually says. "Everyone must be in pairs or a group. There's a chance he won't be at any of the bars tonight. If he is, as soon as you see Kenner, pursue him. We can't let him abduct anyone else and we can't let him get away."

Kelsey looks around, and snorts in disgust. "Where's Jazz?"

Evo frowns as he surveys the room. I admit, I'm a little smug he hadn't noticed her absence. I sure as hell noticed, though; her hatred isn't coating the atmosphere, sucking the fun out of life, and her heavy perfume isn't choking us half to death.

"Earlier, she said she was going to town for some shopping or something," Dyson supplies with a shrug.

194

Kelsey rolls her eyes. "She'll be gone for a while then. I doubt she'll be going with you guys."

"Probably not," Ben mutters and shrugs indifferently. "Though the bars are her thing, I doubt she'd want to help capture this guy. She's never gotten her hands dirty."

"It's probably best that she stays out of it," Flint adds. "She'll slow us down, anyway."

"Guys," Evo warns, putting as much authority behind the unfinished sentence as he can. "That's enough."

Kelsey breathes deep. "If she shows up before you get back, I'll fill her in."

Over the next hour, everyone who is going rehearses all the possible scenarios while I drum my fingers impatiently on the buttons of the remote. After a while, I excuse myself and climb the stairs to our room for a nice, hot shower. I feel grimy from sparring this morning and still have a few spots of dried blood on my face. I also have an errand to run, and if I'm sneaky, I can accomplish it and get back here before anyone notices.

I *need* to meet with the last friend of Cassie's I had planned to interview. My shower is fast and I skip the conditioner entirely. As I towel dry myself, I realize that I need someone to come with me. The friend, Chad, wants to meet outside a bar tonight since he already plans to be there with his friends later this evening. Bre will be a good choice to take, because in the scheme of things, Evo is right. No one should be wandering around alone.

I decide to try my hand with telepathy again while I pick through clothes. *Bre?*

Kenna? She's confused, and rightly so – I have never used telepathy with her before.

Feel like a road trip?

There is a short pause. *Oh, Kenna. . .*

I snort out loud. *Don't. Do you feel like a road trip or not?*

Why?

I have to meet one more friend of Cassie's. The kicker is you can't tell Evo. Not until after we get back. A stretch of silence, and I take it as reluctant confirmation. *Can you be ready in two minutes? I don't want him freaking out and holding me captive. I promise there will be no shenanigans, but I need to talk with this guy.*

Yeah, of course. Where are we going?

I ignore her question. *Dress casual and meet me by the garage.*

Five minutes later, Bre and I are in the SUV grinning ear to ear for sneaking successfully off the territory. No one had run out of the house, and no one had demanded our return. Not yet, anyway. The car races down the long and straight blacktop as we head to the downtown area. Bre drives while we listen to *Too Old To Die Young* by Brother Dege. The lyrics are ironic to our current adventure, and we say nothing as the song booms through the speakers. I can tell she is bursting with questions about where we are headed, though.

As the dark night folds the car into its embrace, I break the silence between us. "How are you doing with this Ben thing?" I ask. "How are you holding up?"

"I'm alright," she responds while keeping her eyes on the road.

"No, you're not," I reply. My tone is matter of fact, chastising for the lie.

"Nope." She pops the 'p' like she always does.

"What are you going to do?"

She scoffs. "What can I do?"

"Well," I draw and turn down the stereo volume. "You could approach him."

"He doesn't know, Kenna. He's all consumed with his beta stuff. It's tempting to approach him, but I want *him* to see *me*. You know, like *actually see me*." She turns a corner and exhales loudly. "To him, I'm just a little side blimp compared to his duties. A wolf who he'll only pay attention to if I'm coming to him with pack stuff. That's all he sees me as."

I sigh and slouch in my seat. "I don't have a romantic bone in my body, so I can't give you solid advice here. The only words of wisdom I have is to give him an ass whooping." She chortles at this. "I'm sure he'll see you then. Preferably when he's bloodied and laying on the floor, wondering what hit him."

"That brings such a tempting scenario in my head. It would get out a lot of frustration I have toward him, too." Still grinning, she shakes her head and tugs at the collar of her sweater. "But it still won't help. I won't force him to see what I'm supposed to be to him."

"Yeah."

"How are you and Evo?" She changes the subject, understandably uncomfortable with discussing her situation.

"Good." I wet my lips. "It's different. I've never had anything like this in my life, so I have nothing to compare it to."

"You've changed a lot since you came here, you know. When you got here, you were all doom and gloom, or whatever."

"Yeah, I sort of was."

I smile when one of my favorite artists comes on. When I start to sing along to *Glitter and Gold* by Barns Courtney, Bre's sad expression morphs to amusement.

"You like Barns Courtney?" she asks, shocked. I can feel her *approval* for my choice in music. I've always loved songs that have a blues or jazz feel to it. Evo says my taste in music is more of a new-age Johnny Cash. Whatever works. Johnny Cash has a special place in my heart, too.

Shuffling my shoulders to the beat, I ignore her question and give her a look that says I don't intend to dance it out in the car all by myself. I'll look like an idiot if I must, but it's much more enjoyable when it's a party of dancing idiots.

Rolling her eyes, she starts to mimic my subtle dance moves and shortly after, begins to sing along with me. By the time we pull into the parking lot of the bar, we are screaming the lyrics with the radio blaring.

I turn down the volume as she guides the SUV into an empty parking spot. Parking, she turns and smiles. "Man, I needed that. The sister I never had."

"I am sort of a big deal," I sniff sarcastically, which makes her laugh.

Through the SUV windows, she looks around at our surroundings, and then frowns. I explain before she questions, "It's the only place I could get him to agree to meet with me. It was hard as hell just to get a hold of him."

A brick building is to our left, and she tips her head toward it. "Are we going in?" She makes a move to exit the car.

"No, he said he would meet us at our car. It's too loud in there to have a normal conversation. His words, not mine." A responsible adult would ask to meet in a quiet setting. Not at a place he intended to get blind drunk at.

"He sounds like a douche," she mutters.

I pull out my phone and dial his number. Before he even answers, he's exits the bar, ringing phone in hand, and scans the parking lot. Hurriedly rolling down the window, I stick my hand out the open space and wave for his attention.

Smiling, he jogs over and bends at the hips to lean and talk through my window.

"'Sup, ladies?" He grins wickedly, an attempt at seductive charm. The youthful man, who barely looks old enough to be in a bar, reeks of beer. Black hair is spiked on top of his head and a tightly fitted back shirt clings to his gangly body.

I roll my eyes. "Chad, this is Bre, a good friend of mine. Bre, this is Chad, Cassie's friend." They both nod to each other. "I'm glad I could catch you. What can you tell me about the night Cassie disappeared?"

He recites the same story I've heard over and over again, complete with wild hand gestures. He claims to have only seen Kenner once. He also admits that he wasn't paying much attention to Cassie the entire night like her girlfriends were. Something about lots of hot ass to grab. It makes me want to smack some maturity into him. That probably won't get me any answers though. *Maybe I can smack him after I get the answers.*

Chad scowls in thought. "I did see the same guy a few nights ago, though."

"Oh, yeah? Where at?" Bre asks.

"Here, at this bar." He points to the brick building behind him. "He was with another girl. I remember because they were all over each other. It was kind of sick. Like seriously, get a room. She was hot, though. Not as hot as you two, but still hot."

I can feel Bre's amusement at this guy. Mentally shrugging, I figure she isn't getting attention from her intended mate at home and is being assaulted by food from another male. I can see the appeal of being found attractive by a complete stranger. However, I don't find this amusing at all. I'm not some piece of ass.

I sigh loudly. "What did the girl look like, Chad? Did he leave with her?"

He shrugs. "She had yellow hair. Preppy. He didn't leave with her, though. She left on her own."

"And then what?" I urge.

"I don't know, dude. After that, my friends showed up and I didn't see him the rest of the night. We were pretty busy." He grins from ear to ear. I roll my eyes. Horny young men – it never fails. "You think that guy took Cassie?"

It's my turn to shrug. "Not sure. Anything else, Chad?"

"Yeah." He smirks. "You two feel like a drink?"

I let my head fall forward as Bre laughs. "No, Chad," I bark. "No, we don't. Some of us have men to get back home to."

"That's too bad," he clicks his tongue and backs away from the car, the rubber heels of his sneakers gritting against pavement. "If you change your mind, I'll be here all night." He winks and takes off back to the bar at a jog.

I shake my head. "Is that guy for real?"

"Kenner has a girlfriend *and* is abducting women?" Bre frowns.

"Sounds like it," I say.

"Ready?" Bre asks, and without waiting for my answer, she reverses the car and we head back to the territory.

CHAPTER TWELVE

Makenna Goldwin

Luckily, we arrived home before anyone had left for the slapped together 'mission.' As soon as we sneak out of the garage, Bre and I go our separate ways. She had drawn the short stick, meaning it was up to her to tell Evo and Ben about Chris' new girlfriend.

I hear her jog toward the alpha quarters while I gnaw on the inside of my cheek, sparing glances at the path in the forest which leads to the pond. Huffing, I decide to take a little detour before heading back into the house. I don't mind one bit that she tells the boys, but Evo's going to be mad that we left without telling anyone in the first place. She's more equipped to handle his tantrum better than I am.

Once I get to the pond, I perch myself against a tree and stare at the water. It's dark, and on the shore, the ducks are tucked into their own feathers while the breeze blows across the surface. I fall into a deep daydream, soaking in an atmosphere that has no one else's emotions flitting about. The next thing I know, I hear Evo lean against the tree next to me. His scent swirls around me, a perfect accent to the pine aroma of the forest.

"I'm surprised you haven't let yet," I mutter. My voice feels too loud surrounded by the quietly sleeping ducks.

"Kelsey wants us to eat first." A rustle of feet against a smooshed pile of last year's autumn leaves. "I know you're upset with me, Kenna," he adds. I am a little surprised he doesn't start off with a lecture, but I'm not going to voice that aloud. He closes the distance and presses his shoulder into the tree my back perches against.

"I am."

"Talk to me."

I adjust my stance to face him, and lightly press my palm to his chest. His heat seeps through and warms my chilled fingers. "I see why it's important that we both don't go. Like you said, if Kenner saw us together before we saw him, there's a good chance he would bolt before we even noticed he was there. *But*, it's still part of my responsibility. Johanna is depending on me."

"I know."

"Did Bre tell you everything?" I shiver at the thought of Chris Kenner having a girlfriend. Who would date this guy? Can't they feel the insanity rolling off him in waves?

He nods. "She did, but there's not much to go on. We still plan to go. If he's at the bar and only sees me with the pack, he should assume it's an outing." Gently, he tucks a piece of hair behind my ear. "I don't want him to have any idea we're mates, Kenna. Nor do I want him aware you're part of the pack. I doubt he even knows you're a wolf. That took me a long time to figure out, myself."

Removing my hand, I arch my back to stretch the stiff muscles along my spine. "I get it, I do." I put my hands on my hips. "But this is my investigation. How am I supposed to just let that go? I was hired to find out what happened to Cassie. I know what happened, but I can't tell Johanna the truth – a wolf snatched her granddaughter up and ate her for breakfast. I could, however, catch Kenner and kill him, ensuring that he never does this again. I wouldn't be able to bring proof to Johanna of what happened to Cassie, but at least I would know the abductions and murders would come to an end."

"Kenna –"

"No. I want justice for Cassie and all his other victims, but I want to be the one to deliver it. Asking me to step aside is something I'm having trouble coping with."

"As do I. But that's not all you're upset about."

The man is too damn perceptive which is inconvenient for me at times like this. I glare up at him. I don't want to admit to anything. But as I

205

stand here, beseeching my mate, my wolf urges me forward, wanting me to continue confiding in him.

I sigh and look away. "If something goes wrong – if something happens and you don't return to me – I don't want to live without you. I don't know if I can." This is true to my deepest level. In such a short amount of time, Evo and the pack have surrounded my life *and* my soul. If I were suddenly at a loss and lost everything, I would be an empty shell. I don't think I could survive such a blow, such a grief. This is a life I never knew existed and never knew I wanted. Now that I have it, I'll never let it go. And if I lose it . . . someone might as well bury me six feet under because I would be a dead man walking. Or woman. Whatever.

"I know," he whispers and then looks up at the moon. It reflects in his blue eyes and highlights gold chips within them. "That's why I'm more than content on keeping you here. This world is new to you. The pack and I . . . this has been our whole lives. We know how to deal with someone like Kenner. If you were there with us, I wouldn't be able to focus right. I need my focus to be on Kenner and not on you. I want to keep you safe." His eyes peer back into mine and my heart skips a beat. "I *need* to keep you safe. If something happened to you, I wouldn't live through it, either. I'd be a robot, simply going through the motions." Lifting a hand, his thumb traces a hot path across my bottom lip.

"Promise me something, Evo."

"M-hmm."

"You know how every story has a hero? And they risk their life for those of others? Don't be that hero."

Evo Johnson

"Thanks, Kelsey," I say as she places the food on the dining table. Lasagna steams from the plates and I inhale the garlicky aroma.

Kenna and I returned from the pond just in time to gather for a late evening meal with the rest of the pack. Everyone is staring with wide grins, looking from Kenna to me, and back again.

While at the pond, Kenna and I had borne our last fear. It was such a simple little fear – the fear of losing each other just after we found one another. It was a great fear, yet simple. Great, because love is a strong and immeasurable force of nature. Simple, because we know neither one of us wants to exist without the other, and we're afraid that possibility will become a reality. Living in a world where your mate could die is something we didn't want to admit to ourselves, let alone say out loud.

I love Kenna, but I didn't know how much I needed her. Not until the possibility of danger came up did I realize how much I needed her. Kenna feels the same. I look at her now, watch as she laughs at something Kelsey said. Guilt worms its way into my gut for keeping information from her – information that was in the folder Ben had given me. *Information that can wait,* I tell myself.

Out in the woods and under the witness of the moon and stars, we felt the need to be close to each other. That need turned into an uncontrollable desire, and we had sex one last time, a physical promise unlike any other.

I cut into a wide noodle as the memory of our joining replays in my head. Unlike our normal frantic romps, tonight was slow and steady. She had called my name like a whispering breeze, her back against the bank of the pond while I took my time sliding in and out of her. Kenner had been pushed from my mind entirely.

Now, a small part of me hopes we don't see Kenner tonight. Hopes that he crawled in some small hole and is withering away his useless, pathetic little life. I could return to my mate, the possibility of danger a little less than was before. That would just be too easy though, wouldn't it?

Kenna places her hand over mine when she feels me getting angry through the direction of my thoughts. I turn to my mate and smile, eyes tracing the puffy claiming mark on her neck.

By the pond, we both had been moaning when an overwhelming urge had overcome me. My wolf was pushing for the surface. Not to take over, but to share the space with me. I've never had that feeling before and it was shocking. I can easily call upon his claws and teeth, but it was never anything more than that. It's always ever been either him or me in control. This time wasn't like that.

When I had opened my eyes, Kenna's glowing wolf eyes were on mine, her canines elongated, and her claws formed. I knew what was happening then, and instinctually, my body began to respond in the same manner.

I had asked her, a little muffled when I tried to talk around my elongated canines, if she knew what was happening. She didn't, and she had looked a little frightened.

"It's the mating," I said. "Our wolves are pushing us to claim one another. The mating is progressing. This will be the last step, if you're ready to take it with me."

I wouldn't allow the claiming unless it was something she was sure of. I wanted her to be ready to fully accept me and our destiny – our fate – together. When she nodded, I had groaned with relief and slammed into her. She was ready to be all mine and it had heightened my arousal. We had let our instinct take over, and my wolf provided direction.

Hand cupped under the nape of her neck, I lunged forward and bit into the soft flesh, my wolf growling in satisfaction as he shared my space with me, completing his part of the mating. She screamed at the pleasure and bite of pain, enduring an orgasm at the same time. I could hear her heart beat frantically at the reaction from my wolf's bite. It was changing her, completing the mating and making us one.

So fast I had barely caught the movement, she bit into my neck. The pleasure was beyond what I had imagined it to be, filling my body with such heat. The snap inside my heart was startling, and then it began to beat frantically as it matched Kenna's. I could feel a space bloom inside my head that was meant solely for Kenna. Her undiluted happiness and love for me filled this space. It was a pleasant surprise. I knew she loved me, but to *feel it* . . .

Having reached my climax, I had come inside her so hard that I saw stars behind my eyelids. I desperately fought to stay conscious. Kenna however – I felt her slump to the bank as she fainted. I hadn't worried. It's normal for some to faint as the sensation is so overwhelming and powerful in its own right.

The memory fades and I breathe a sigh of content. I stab my cut noodle and shove the lasagna in my mouth. I can feel her love for me, just as I can feel the pack's excitement that their alphas have completed the mating.

For some wolves, it can take months, or years, to complete a mating. On a rare occasion, it will only take days. It's a relief to know that not only does the pack find joy in our mating, but it hadn't taken as long as they were expecting – as we all were expecting.

When we completed the mating, her gift became mine too. It's no longer her burden to bear alone. When an emotion reaches me, it's a strange sensation that sweeps over my skin like a breeze. It's something I'm going to have to get used to, but at the moment, I find it entertaining and interesting.

I can really learn a lot about someone by how they are feeling. Gone are the days of dishonesty. I find this new gift intriguing and can't wait to learn more about how it works. But that isn't the only thing I find fascinating.

As I can feel her in her own space inside my mind, I can also detect her heartbeat. It matches my own, speeds and slows together. When she's excited and her rate accelerates, mine does as well. If we can feed off each other like this now, I can't wait to see what it's like during sex.

Knowing what I am thinking, or maybe feeling, her smile rearranges into a glare. I can feel her annoyance toward me for thinking of sex while we're eating.

I lean over, peck my prickly mate on the cheek, then seductively touch the tip of my tongue to my eyetooth. She stops chewing. Her eyes glow wolf for a moment, and her lust slams into me. I smile at her in triumph, and shove more lasagna in my mouth. I can't wait to spend the rest of my life with my little spitfire. She's so easily provoked. So responsive.

Feeling an odd sensation spread over my skin, I stop chewing as I try to place it – to give it a name. It's going to take a while for me to get used to this gift Kenna now shares with me. It isn't easy placing an emotion with its name.

Anger, I realize with a blink. The feeling is anger. I look over my pack mates. Flint and Dyson are still grinning like fools at their alphas. Ben's entire dish is consumed and he's slouched in his chair, patting his stomach. Kelsey, Bre, and Jeremy have moved on and are already talking about a different topic. I feel nothing unusual from any of them.

I watch as Bre picks at her food, nodding distractedly to Kelsey while stealing glances of Ben. I can feel her jealousy for Kenna and me. It isn't about us, per say. I know that. Instead, it's for what we have that she doesn't. I can feel her *deep longing* for the one she loves.

I suck in a quiet breath. Of course, she loves Ben. Oh, what a tangled web that's been weaved. I'm going to have to tuck that away for further investigation.

In the corner of my vision, I notice Kenna's visibly pressing her tongue to the inside of her teeth, trying to actively ignore the Bre and Ben situation. I gather that she knows all about it. After all, she's dealt with this gift her entire life. I'm a little surprised she hasn't voiced the Bre and Ben issue to me, though. Surprised, but not upset. My mate's loyalty to my sister is astonishing. Pride wells in my chest, and I know, without a doubt, she's the greatest addition to this pack we've ever had. I wonder if she knows that.

Her emotions spike until her annoyance pricks against my tongue.

Frowning, I follow her new line of sight to Jazz down the table. She had arrived at the house unexpectedly while Kenna and I were at the pond, and from there, Kelsey had kept her word and caught her up on this evening's plans.

Jazz isn't eating her meal; instead, she's watching the pack from under long false lashes. I can feel Jazz's anger ripple down the surface of the table, though I can't place the reason for it. I can also feel her anticipation, but again, I can't place the reason. This gift seems to have its limits, and rightfully so.

I shovel another bite in my mouth and chew thoughtfully. Jazz, Kenna, and I are going to have to sit down and have a discussion. I doubt Kenna, being an alpha and a queen alpha at that, will put up with Jazz's hostility for much longer. At some point, my mate will end up challenging her. As much as I know it's her right to do so, I would hate to see one of our wolves be further outcast from our pack. Something like that could make Jazz turn rogue.

Deciding to worry about that later, I tuck that idea beside the conversation I plan to have with Brenna. I need to have a clear head for tonight. These aren't immediate issues and can be dealt with tomorrow.

Kenna finishes her wine and sets her wine glass back on the table. I watch as Jazz takes notice, stands from her seat, and walks into the kitchen. She quickly returns with the wine bottle, red liquid sloshing and condensation dripping down the sides.

Frowning, I watch as she walks over to Kenna and fills her cup. The bitter scent of the wine fills the air. Kenna watches with narrowed eyes, but Jazz beams and shallowly bows her head. I can still feel her hatred for Kenna, but I can also detect an odd sensation of relief. These emotions don't add up to a grand gesture such as this.

Kenna is close to snapping at Jazz. The chatter seizes as everyone anticipates a spat to unfold at any moment. Ducking their chins, the pack tries to make their gawking as unnoticeable as possible. They're just as confused as I am. Why would Jazz take it upon herself to refill her alpha's cup when we all damn well know Jazz and Kenna despise one another?

I put my hand at the back of Kenna's nape, a reassuring touch and wordless warning. Now isn't the time or place for something disastrous to unfold.

She understands my gesture, straightens her shoulders, and nods a reluctant thanks to Jazz. When Jazz walks away, Kenna takes a sip of her wine and then looks at me questioningly.

I frown at the kitchen where Jazz disappeared to.

I don't know, I send Kelsey telepathically, answering her unasked question.

I have no idea what Jazz is up to. But again, it is something to solve tomorrow. Maybe early in the morning, if Jazz is going to keep pretending to be nice to get on Kenna's nerves. Jazz has to have no idea she is playing with fire.

Putting all of this aside, I begin tuning into the pack's renewed conversation.

"We should have a bonfire again," Jeremy suggests. He turns to me. "We haven't had one for at least a year."

"Yes!" Dyson shouts and thumps his fist against the table. "I could get out the sound system and bring it to the yard. We could play music and roast marshmallows." At our blinks of shock to his outburst, he shrugs. "It could be a thing."

"After we take down Chris." Ben points his fork at Dyson.

Dyson rests his hand over his heart and fakes hurt for being scolded. "But, Dad!"

Kenna chuckles when Ben frowns.

"What about fishing?" Flint suggests through a mouth full of saucy lasagna. "We could go fishing. The creatures of the pond need to be thinned out. You fish, Kenna?

"Not unless I'm forced to," she says grumpily. I smile at her. I understand her aversion to it. I just don't have the patience to sit in one spot all day and stare at a pole.

"How about not," Bre says, mirroring Kenna's attitude. "When was the last time we went for a pack run? We could do that instead of fish."

Now that the pack is complete with two alphas, the atmosphere of the pack itself is brimming with anticipation. It's only natural that they want to do things together as a whole. I tip back in my chair, arms folded behind my head, and smile.

"What about you, Ben?" I ask. "What's on your to-do list?"

"I'd like to add on to the gym," he says after a moment of thought. "Maybe put down some mats and hang some mirrors so we can spar in there. It wouldn't be a bad idea to start some Krav Maga since we are earning some enemies." He looks at me pointedly.

I learned Krav Maga in the FBI and had taught Ben when I became alpha. At the beginning, it was frustrating to teach, but eventually, it was rewarding.

Ben's past isn't something we reflect on often, but he used to have a terrible temper. He couldn't control himself and would often smash his fist into the wall when his emotions became too much for his body to contain. He was wild. An untamed youth. Krav Maga helped him soothe his anger and harness his energy into something else – his duties as beta. It gave him purpose and he started living again.

Now, in no way, shape, or form, will I ever question if Ben can hold his own. We haven't started teaching the rest of the pack yet, though it's been discussed. Both of us had agreed their strength was first priority.

Brenna snorts at Ben. "You would." I blink to the hostility of her tone.

"That's not a bad idea," I supply, doing my best to ignore Brenna's irritation. Now that the pack financials are improving, we can afford to renovate.

"You think the Gray Pack will actually retaliate?" Kelsey asks as she brings a fresh pan of garlic

Texas toast to the table. Everyone thanks her as they grab a second helping.

"I do. The alpha was pissed when I wouldn't let him deal with this on his own."

Kenna frowns while looking around. "Where the hell did Jazz go?"

"She was just in the kitchen. Told me she was headed out," Kelsey explains while perching herself on the edge of the table.

"What the fuck? She really plans on not helping the pack tonight?" Kenna asks.

"Of course, she isn't," Kelsey replies, gracefully nibbling on a piece of garlic toast. Even though she looks calm, cool, and collected, I can feel her anger at Jazz, just like the rest of the pack.

"I'll have a talk with her tomorrow morning," I say.

CHAPTER THIRTEEN

Makenna Goldwin

I sit on the porch swing with Kelsey. Together, we watch the pack drive away while sipping the rest of supper's wine. Crickets chirp from the shadows and Jeremy's eyes glow bright green from inside the forest. Bre's white wolf is somewhere out there, too.

Swirling the contents, I sigh with displeasure. "I don't like seeing my mate leave pack territory without me," I mutter. *Especially when he's off to do some wolf hunting.* It doesn't sit well with me at all, and all throughout helping Kelsey with dishes, it had been the only thing occupying my mind.

"How does it feel to be mated?" Kelsey asks, trying to distract me as I continue to watch where the cars have disappeared.

I turn, angling my body to face hers. "Different, but in a very good way. I can feel him in my mind and heart. It's indescribable." I snort. "He's loving my gift, though. I could see it on his face and feel it right here." I tap my temple. "Empathy is going to be his new hobby; I just know it."

Kelsey laughs.

Being mated to Evo is more than I expected. Even now, with the distance between us, his heartbeat matches my own. A reassuring *thump, thump, thump.* I look to the woods where Jeremy's wolf was standing, now gone. I can feel Evo's mood and emotions, too. They're seemingly chattering in a tiny pocket of my mind that belongs only to him. He doesn't feel right about leaving me either.

"That's exactly what I tell people when they ask me what it's like – that it's indescribable, because it is." She traces her finger around the rim of her wine cup. "How do you describe two people meshing together to be one?"

I nod. "You can't know unless you experience it firsthand."

Her eyes drift to my neck where the claiming mark is. It still throbs a little. "Did you faint?" At my blush, she laughs. "Don't feel embarrassed. Jeremy fainted, too."

I laugh with her as a mental picture forms. I can see her trying to slap Jeremy awake, too. It would be just like her to do that.

Unexpected exhaustion hits me, and I yawn. I take another sip of wine, hoping the chill of the alcohol chases it away. I have no plans to go to bed before

Evo gets back. I don't want to wait until morning to hear what happened and I want to be awake to *feel* him in case something does happen. My shoulders slump as I blink hard.

Maybe just a little nap. A small one. My blinks slow.

I feel concern come from Kelsey.

"Don't worry, honey." She pats my thigh. "They'll be alright. There's four of them and only one of Chris. Even if Chris is a crazy rogue, he's still no match for any one of them."

"And what about the girlfriend?" I ask sleepily. I pinch the bridge of my nose. My vision is blurring. Or is that the night playing tricks on my mind?

"If she's human, Evo will get her out of the way. He'll probably use the alpha's command or something. If she's another wolf, they'll just bring her back here and decide what to do with her. But first, they'll want to find out who she is and where she came from."

I nod, empty my wine, and glare inside the cup.

She frowns and takes it from me. "Are you okay?"

"Just tired."

"Do you need some coffee?"

"Oh, you know the way to my heart, don't you?" I smile weakly up at her as she stands from the porch swing and makes her way into the house.

Seeing Jeremy's wolf dart cross the lawn and enter the other side of the woods, I let my head fall back and close my eyes for a minute. *Just a minute. A little nap.*

Jumping at the sound of glass shattering in the house, I turn and look into the window behind me. "You okay, Kelsey?" I squint, trying to get my eyes to focus past the living room couch.

When she doesn't answer, I hoist myself off the swing and shuffle to open the door. "Shit," I grunt. My world spins and I tilt with it. I grip the door's frame tightly as I struggle with my legs. They don't want to function. Instead, needles and spikes prick their way down the nerves.

"What the hell?" I whisper, then groan as another wave of dizziness makes me sway.

Gritting my teeth, I stumble inside. "Kelsey, something's wrong." She doesn't answer. "Kelsey?"

Silence.

I hold onto the wall as I make my way into the kitchen. My blurry vision lands on the shards of a broken mug and a puddle of steaming dark brew. I stop dead.

"Kelsey? You okay?"

I don't see blood, but I smell it. For a moment, I think maybe her absence is because she cut herself trying to pick up the pieces of the coffee cup. If there are no visible droplets of blood, that can't be a correct assumption. Where the hell is she?

A phantom weight presses my shoulders down, the exhaustion a life of its own as it settles heavy in my joints. I use everything to aid my balance. Pictures fall from the wall and potted plants tip over. Each step is taken like a newborn calf.

Fumbling around the corner and into the dining room, I come to another halt. "Jazz?"

In the dim light, Jazz has an unconscious Kelsey tied to a chair and a gun held to her head. The bitch smiles at me.

A distant canine yelp from outside. I spare only a glance at the sliding glass door but see nothing beyond pitch black night. That's when realization hits my sluggish mind.

"You spiked my wine," I slur, and her grin widens.

Oh, God. The blood from the gash on Kelsey's forehead drips and splats on the floor. The distant yelp – that was Jeremy, probably making his way back to the house when he felt Kelsey's pain through their mating bond. *We're under attack.*

"You aren't here alone," I say, swaying. My back bumps against the wall and it takes all my strength to keep my head up and my feet under me. "What the fuck are you doing?"

Unable to hold myself upright any longer, my body slides to the floor. I try to contact Evo telepathically, but the sedative makes it impossible to get through.

My heart thuds once in fear. There's no way I can defend myself, Kelsey, Jeremy, Bre, and the territory in my current state. I am fighting hard enough just to stay conscious.

Where is Bre? Is she hurt, too? I grunt a moan and blink blurry up at Jazz. I won't be able to contact Bre if I can't contact Evo. What if it's worse? What if she's dead?

I roll my head as if the drug my tip out of my ears. "You bitch. What the fuck did you give me?"

"You're right, I am." Jazz giggles. "How's that wine treating you, princess? It's my special little blend. I added it just for you."

"Why are you doing this?"

Switching the gun to her other hand, she continues to smile at me. "Well, you see, Evo was my ticket to be alpha female and you took that from me. I've been denied what's mine and I want it back. Now, I'm going to have the entire pack watch as I take it for myself. Starting with ridding the pack of you." She cocks her head to the side and clicks her tongue. "Not much of a queen, now are you?"

"That's a mighty plan you have there – drugging me to even the odds. A real genius, you are." I adjust my seat with difficulty. "You're aware that you have to be an alpha to run a pack, right? Who plans to help you with your fantasies? Who are you working with?"

She points the gun at me as the back porch's glass door swishes open and closed. Someone walks into the dining room. My tired eyes blink slowly at a male's fine leather shoes grinding against the floor as whoever it is approaches. He bends down and familiarly wicked ice-blue eyes bore into mine.

My hatred roars and I can feel my wolf trying to find the strength to surface and defend, but she can't muster any more energy than I can. I can't even move my limbs to kill the sick bastard a few inches from my face.

"Kenner," I mutter. *Shit.* At this point, my only hope is to bide my time until either the drug wears off or someone comes to the rescue.

"Now can we kill her?" Jazz hisses.

"Not yet, Jazzy, my love. Remember? I tried brute force and the vampire failed. A direct attack doesn't work." Still in a squat, he swivels and peers up at Jazz. "Besides, you promised I'd get to have a little fun first."

"My love?" I chortle but it sounds more like I'm choking. "What? Are you two psychos a team?" Realization dawns on me and my mouth slackens. "You're the girlfriend."

"Girlfriend?" She snarls at me. "He's my mate, you bitch."

My shock is genuine, and I shake my head in small successions. Jazz pulls her hooded sweatshirt away from her neck and exposes her claiming mark as evidence. The mating is complete. *Shit. Double shit.*

"You two are a match made in heaven," I say sarcastically, fighting to keep it above a whisper. The drugs are beginning to take me under. I can't be unconscious. Not now, with crazy Barbie-bitch and cannibal fuck-tard in the same room as me.

"Mmm," Kenner purrs. "But we are, aren't we, darling." He bends down and picks up my arm. Fingers painfully tight, he yanks me away from the wall and drags me across the floor. I grunt as he roughly hoists me in the chair next to Kelsey's. He kneels in front of me once more. "I've heard you haven't been nice to my mate."

"I'm not known for good manners."

Smirking, he takes the offered chair from Jazz and sits at eye level with me. Next, he handles a leather flap folded like a rolled tortilla, and places it on the table.

I weakly growl as Jazz grabs my arms and wraps them around the back of my chair, tying them tightly together at the wrists. "What are you doing?" I ask, but my question goes unanswered. This isn't going to be good.

Kenner unrolls the leather flap. At the sight of his shiny tools being exposed, my heart rate thuds faster, fear coursing through my veins as my wolf tries frantically to muster an ounce of strength.

Keep them talking. Keep. Them. Talking.

"What exactly is your idea of fun?" I try to lift my limbs to see if I can try to escape this, but they aren't even twitching. My voice is barely above a whisper as it is.

Kenner sighs as he lines his tools up neatly. "I must admit, it was a surprise to learn you were a wolf. But it's of no matter." He waves his hand in the air. "You've been a particularly difficult woman to kill, Makenna. After sending the vampire after you, you went off the radar. That is, until I met my Jazzy at a bar in town. She had all sorts of information on you. In fact, my darling is the one who came up with this idea. She knew your pack would soon be out searching for me, and when that opportunity came, I would slip in, take care of you, and give my mate what she wants – to be alpha. At the same time, I get what I want. By killing you, I'll be killing your mate." He holds what looks to be a scalpel up to the light. The tiny sharp edge glints. "Two birds, one stone. And when I'm finished with you, I'll kill Kelsey and . . . Who was the wolf outside?"

"Jeremy," Jazz spits.

"Right. I'll kill him, too. No witnesses."

"You really think this pack will listen to Jazz?" I spare a glance at the sliding glass door, fighting the urge to ask about Bre. Kenner hasn't mentioned her yet. Jazz must have forgotten about her. With every hope that Bre is still out there, I know she is my only chance at this point. Kelsey doesn't look to be waking any time soon, and she'll be in absolutely no shape to figure a way out of here, either.

The scalpel handle settles in his palm. I frantically think of ways to distract these loons long enough to live, because that simple little knife looks mightily sharp. I'm not naive enough to think that I'm not about to go through a world of pain. But knowing if I die, Evo will die with me . . .

I have to come up with something to gain more time. Evo can't die. I just can't imagine a world without him in it. This pack needs him. To fall under the hands of these two sadistic fucks would be a tragedy.

"Oh, they'll listen," he says cheerfully. "Or die. Whichever they prefer. Personally, I hope they pick the latter. I have a new flay knife I'm dying to try out."

Goosebumps rise on my skin at his palpable glee. "It doesn't have to be this way, Chris. You've found your mate. You two can go start your own pack and be happy. No one has to die."

He looks at me thoughtfully. "I like Jazz's idea much better. Her way sounds more . . . exciting." He turns to Jazz at my side. "Is she secure, darling?"

"Yes." The purred word makes me want to vomit. They are well suited for each other. Psycho and Psycho.

"What did you do with all the people you abducted?" I question, trying to keep this guy's attention off carving me up like a Halloween pumpkin.

"I believe you already know the answer to that, little queen." At my shock, he laughs. "Yes, I know about that. My Jazzy doesn't keep things from me. Including everything said or speculated about me within your pack."

Between my drugged body and the confirmed suspicions on what Chris was doing with the people he abducted, my stomach rolls. *He is eating people*. Actually eating them. It's one thing to suspect, but a whole other situation to have it confirmed.

"And you're okay with this?" I ask Jazz. "Are you hopping on the cannibal train, too?" She doesn't answer me.

Chris slaps his knee. "Now, Makenna. Did you know my favorite color is red? Not a normal red. I enjoy the color that comes from a deep vein." He lets the scalpel tickle the skin on my arm.

My breath quickens at the impending pain. "Don't. Please."

"The dark red – it's such a soothing color, don't you think?"

"Don't!"

"It tastes so lovely and slides down the tongue with such a slick ease."

He slowly presses the knife into my upper arm. A scream bubbles in my chest. It splits my skin and he drags it halfway down my arm. I clench my teeth and moan my pain. My wolf musters up snarls inside my head, angry that she can't be set free. I can feel the warm blood trailing paths down my pinky. The *drip, drip, drip* of it splattering to the floor makes my stomach heave.

Not wanting to watch myself be butchered, I scrunch together my eyelids until I feel the blade lift from my flesh. I pant and swallow, ignoring the scent of iron heavy in the air and the feel of Kenner's ravenous hunger.

"See that color, Jazzy, darling?" he eventually says. "Isn't it as beautiful as I said it would be?" He touches his finger to the flow of blood and brings it to his lips, tasting. I watch as his eyes glow wolf and he hums as it slides across his tongue.

"You're a sick fuck."

"Insulting me will get you nowhere, Makenna." Those words are the same words I had told Evo the first night I met him as Chris was being escorted from the police station. He had heard them, and now he's throwing them back at me.

Eyes still glowing, he pierces the skin on my other arm, creating the same injury. I'm not prepared and scream as soon as the first blood wells. He pays no attention to my hollered pleas. He's completely consumed with the taste of my blood.

Evo Johnson

"This place is a madhouse," Dyson screams over the music.

The pound of its beat, the swirl of the strobe lights, the ever-moving swell and flow of dancing bodies, and the assault of so many emotions – it dulls all my senses until I no longer know where I begin and where I end.

I clutch my head. I don't know how Kenna does this and stays sane. No wonder she used to live on her own. Nobody with this gift would live with a group of humans.

We have only just entered the bar and fanned out in pairs. Ben and Flint are on the other side of the bar's island, Flint flirting with a gold-dusted short skirt, and Dyson and I sit on stools closest to the main entrance. If we have any hope of catching Chris, our best bet is to stay near the entrance. Unless he's already here, which is why Ben and Flint are on the other side. Chris should order a drink or two if he plans to blend in. That's the hope, anyway.

I drum my fingers against the wet bar top. It is a good system, but the problem is that locating Chris in this massive flow of people may prove to be difficult. It would be a perfect place for him to find a victim while remaining hidden.

Unsuspectingly, my heart begins thudding faster, a surge of misplaced adrenaline, and my wolf is startled by it, pacing inside me. I clutch at my chest, unsure if it's me, or someone else's emotions bombarding mine.

"You okay?" Dyson asks.

I nod, rub my sternum one more time, and spare a glance at Flint and Ben. They haven't moved, and Ben shakes his head at my questioning look. He hasn't seen Chris yet.

Exhaling a deep breath, I straighten my spine and shake off the odd sensation. The adrenaline is either a horny immature youth, or my anxiety desperate to get this over with and get back to Kenna. I blink. *But my heart wasn't pounding before now.* My wolf wasn't this anxious before now, either. He's usually calm and confident before any form of challenge.

"How are we going to find him in here?" Dyson asks.

"Just keep your eyes open. He may not even be here. There are plenty of bars in town with plenty of people to snatch."

"How do we even know he plans to go out tonight?"

"We don't." I grind my teeth. This is all by guess. However, we can't sit at home any longer and pretend he isn't out here abducting women, potentially exposing our race. If the police catch him before we do, more people will get hurt and our entire way of life will be uprooted. It would be disastrous.

Just the thought of him abducting another woman makes me glad I left Kenna at home where she's safe. I search the corner of my mind which now belongs to her. I told myself I wouldn't keep tabs on her while we were out here looking for Chris, but I can't hold back from doing so anymore.

I frown as my wolf growls. Kenna's heart rate is accelerated. It beats far faster than it should, and I can taste her potent fear which drives it. It explains my own bodily changes.

Kenna, what's wrong? I send telepathically. I wait for her to respond but get nothing. The bar top groans under my constricting grip.

Dyson takes in my rigid posture. "Evo?"

The stool tips over as I stand abruptly. Pushing through the crowd waiting for their orders to be taken, I quickly stride the remaining distance to the door. I shoulder it open and the brisk night air stuffs up my nose.

Fists clenched at my sides, I search again, hoping I had simply misread her emotions. I feel her fear. A whole lot of fear. My muscles quiver with the urge to shift. I whip around and face Dyson who had followed me out.

"What is it, Evo?" Dyson demands, he releases the door's handle and it softly closes, effectively smothering the boom of the bar's music.

The silence last for only a second though, as the door slams open again and Flint and Ben rush outside. Taking in my expression, they stiffen with tension. Before they can ask what's going on, I say, "We have to go. Now!"

Without questions, Ben fishes the keys from his pocket and throws them at me. We run to the SUV parked in the middle of the sea of cars. I hop in on the driver's side, huffing with adrenaline.

"Damn it, Evo. What's going on?" Ben asks, holding onto the safety handle as I peel out of the parking lot.

"Something's wrong at the house. Kenna's terrified."

"Can't you just ask her?" Flint asks, referring to the telepathy.

"I tried that," I growl. I turn a corner and the tires squeal.

"What about everyone else on the territory? Did you try them?"

Shit. No, I didn't think of that. Flexing my jaw to force myself to concentrate, I reach out to Jeremy, Kelsey, then Jazz, and get nothing. Not a single response. Lastly, I reach out to Brenna.

Brenna? My mind's voice is panicked.

Yeah?

The steering wheel groans as I grip it tighter. *What the hell is going on at the house?*

I don't know what's going on at the house – I'm running patrol with Jeremy, but it sounded like Jeremy got injured. I'm on my way to see if he's okay.

I blink one second and press further down on the gas the next. *Brenna, no! Something is going on at the house. Check that first. Something's wrong with Kenna.*

Are you sure I shouldn't check on Jeremy first? Her voice is skeptical. *You know how clumsy he can be. Last I checked, Kenna and Kelsey were on the front porch.*

Just do it, damn it.

Okay, okay! Geez, Evo. Give me a few minutes.

I feel selfish that I want her to check on Kenna first. But if we are under attack, the attackers will go after the alpha. Kenna is the only alpha home. I push the car faster as my fear begins to take over. It could very well be George and his wolves, and if he finds out who Kenna is . . .

"Words, Evo. Use your words," Ben says.

"Jeremy, Kelsey, and Jazz aren't responding. Brenna is the only one who answered, and she said she heard Jeremy get hurt. I sent her to the house to check on Kenna first."

A slicing pain rips through my arm. "Fuck!" I accidentally tug at the steering wheel and the car swerves across the dotted line. I look down at my arm, but there's nothing but normal, unmarred skin. My wolf howls inside my head as realization hits me.

"What the hell!" Dyson barks, righting himself from being tipped over into Flint's lap.

"I think Kenna's hurt." I push the car even faster, racing back to the territory. Speed limits be damned.

Evo! Chris and Jazz –

"Chris?" I say out loud. The three in the car echo the name. *Did you say Chris? Chris Kenner?*

Yes! Shut up and listen! They have Kenna and Kelsey. Kelsey isn't conscious and I can't tell if she's injured from where I stand. But Kenna . . . Evo, they have her strapped to a chair and he's cutting into her.

I growl and I know without looking that my eyes were glowing wolf. My wolf is fighting for the surface and I'm struggling to reason with him. He won't be able to get there faster than the SUV.

I slam the heel of my palm against the center council. Why didn't I see this coming? Pieces begin sliding together. Jazz's behavior and her trips to town alone. Chris' absence in abductions. Of course, they are working together. I am going to kill them both.

What's going on, Brenna? I push for more information.

He's cutting her, Evo, she says again, an agonizing tone as I feel another slice of pain on the other arm. *There's blood. A lot of blood. Evo, what do you want me to do?*

I breathe through the pain, spittle flying from my lips and tears streaming down my cheeks. Chris had moved on from my arms and began on my calves. Blood puddles around my chair and slopes until it disappears under the table. At this rate, I'm going to bleed to death. I'm running out of time and I know it. Even now, I can feel my heart rate slow as a chill settles into my muscles.

I am out of ideas for distractions. He's no longer entertaining my questions, too consumed in tasting my blood. Trying to use Evo – who I can feel is in a blind panic – as an anchor, I force myself to keep my eyes open. In the position my head is slumped, the only thing I can see is the blood. The blood, the deep gash down the side of my leg, and the tips of Jazz's shoes.

"One more, Makenna, and then I'll kill you. I'm sure you'll prove to be the most delicious meal. I'll remove your head one slice at a time." He draws a finger across my neck, a finger coated in my blood.

"It'll make a great centerpiece for the dining table," Jazz spits.

"That doesn't sound sanitary," I croak.

"And once it's removed," he continues, as if he hadn't heard a word. "I'll peel back your skin and flay the flesh from the bone."

My will to fight is strong, but my body is growing even weaker. The struggle to stay conscious is becoming a losing battle. I can already feel a weight beginning to pull me under, feel my connection to Evo slip away.

I'm not going to show Kenner fear, even though fear is coursing through my veins and the tears of my pain splat against my shirt. I don't want to die. Not when my life has just begun.

I brace myself and hold my breath as he brings his scalpel down to make another slice along my leg. A window crashes to the floor at the front of the house and a fierce growl rips through the air, vibrating off the walls.

"Shit," Jazz hisses. At the sound of clothes ripping, I raise my weak eyes speckled with growing black dots. Chris jumps out of his chair and the scalpel clatters to the floor, splashing in my blood. Chris and Jazz began transforming into their wolf halves.

Just before the black takes me under and swallows me whole, I see Evo's wolf tackle Chris' partially transformed body. Bre's white wolf leaps and Jazz screams. The sound of vicious snarling and snapping begins to fade as the black fully descends.

The blackness is calming, warm to my cold shaking body. I hadn't realized I was shaking, quivering like a leaf braced against the wind. Mentally, I moan as the black folds around me.

CHAPTER FOURTEEN

Makenna Goldwin

Beep. Beep. Beep.

My eyelids flutter open to the steady beat of a high-pitched sound, pulling me from a deep, dreamless sleep. I can smell chemicals, and I'm just about to stretch my stiff neck when a hand gently presses on my arm. I flinch at the sudden unexpected touch, my entire arm sensitive and bruised.

Evo stares down at me, a relieved smile playing at the corner of his lips. He looks exhausted, and his hair is standing on end as if he'd been tugging on it for hours. Or days?

"How are you feeling, baby?" he reaches and brushes a warm finger against my cold cheek.

I shut my heavy eyes for a moment, curious to the reasoning of his question. The beeps – I am surrounded by medical equipment. Wiggling my fingers, I can feel the tape on my hand from an I.V. Am I in a hospital? Had I died?

Searching my mind for the last thing I remember, it comes back in full force. I blink and stare at my arms covered in white bandages and tape. My legs are covered with our thick comforter which answers my question – we are home. My room. *Our room.*

More questions scrunch my features.

The mattress dips as Evo sits on the side of the bed. "Chris is dead," he begins. "And Jazz managed to escape. We haven't been able to find her yet, but I don't want you to worry. We'll find her." His voice is flat with barely contained anger.

"But they're mates," I croak. She should be dead right along with him.

He pushes hair from my forehead. "Remember the story I told you about my parents? How the mating bond didn't form a full puzzle?" I nod against my pillow. "We think that's what happened."

"Chris was too rogue to fully bond."

He studies my face and switches the subject. "How are you feeling?"

I glance around. Light splashes across the floor, bashing shadows from every corner of our room. The reclining chair is pulled up next to our bed, and a pillow and blanket sit on the floor beside it. Under the bedroom door, I can see several shadows moving, pacing, and hear the quiet whispers of my pack.

I lift one of my arms and wince when at the pull of stitches. "A little sore, but I'll live. How long was I out for?"

Evo frowns at my disregard for my own pain. I can feel how worried he is, and how much he is trying to keep himself together. It must have been scary for him.

"Two days."

I spare him a glance. "Was it bad?"

He runs a finger across his eyebrow. "You almost died. I could feel you slipping away."

I grasp his other hand in mine. "I'm sorry."

His lips find mine and softly brush against them. "You can't ever do that to me again. I don't think I could survive the stress of seeing you injured and almost dying again."

My mind flashes back. I remember going in and out of consciousness when the pack carried me up to the room. There was a lot of shouting. A lot of panic. I remember Evo trying to talk to me, but I couldn't focus on what he was saying at that time. I remember the jostling as my clothes were ripped off, and the piles of white hand towels drenched in blood.

"Well, that wasn't my intention, I assure you." I roll my shoulders. "The bitch drugged me. My entire body wouldn't work right. How did you get all this medical crap in here? Who brought all this stuff?"

Evo looks at all the machines. "One of the Riva Pack shifters is a doctor. They were kind enough to lend her to us. We were lucky. *You* were lucky. She was just leaving work at a hospital when we called her. It's not too far from here." He snaps the wrinkles from the comforter. I can tell he is reliving everything that happened through his mind.

"Are you okay?" I whisper.

He tenses and avoids my gaze. "Kenna, what happened?"

I explain everything to him. From the drugged wine, to the confirmed suspicions, up until he arrived. He remains silent as I explain everything, but I keep the painful things to myself. The *things* I'll have to deal with on my own. I won't burden him further. Not after this. Not while knowing he'll have his own demons to contend with, too.

"Jazz and Chris were mates," he says in a sighing breath. He runs a hand through his hair. "That explains why she would be okay with attacking her own pack."

"How so?"

"She was probably on her way to becoming as rogue as Chris was. Chris' mental state of mind wouldn't have been able to give himself entirely over to the bond, but if Jazz gave all of herself, then she would become just as rogue as he was. She had to have known for a little while now that they were mates and kept it from us, probably at his request."

"So, by fully handing herself to him, the crazier she became."

"It's driving me nuts that I never really saw how different she had become. And when I did notice something was up, I ignored it. If I hadn't shoved her behavior off at the dinner table the other night, I could have solved all of this before it even started."

"You're not the only one who shoved off her behavior." I run my finger over a piece of tape holding the gauze down by my wrist. "Even though I don't know her like you guys do, I had ignored my instincts when it came to her. I should have known better, too. But there's nothing we can do about it now. It's over and done with." I look back to him. "Are you sure Jazz is still alive?"

Evo sighs. "I didn't feel her death in the pack link. Only her severing the ties. Wherever she's going, she'll be physically weak for a long time. I haven't been able to contact her for a while – not even when we were driving back from the bar. She had to have been slowly cutting the connection to our pack for days for me to not notice any of her plans."

"Is Kelsey alright? Jeremy? What about Bre?" I try to sit up, but Evo gently keeps me from doing so with a hand to my shoulder.

"They're all fine. Kelsey has a few stitches but doesn't remember anything. Brenna doesn't have a scratch on her. Jeremy had hit his head when he got trapped in a net, but he's completely unharmed. Extremely pissed, but fine."

"I'm sure he's angrier about his mate."

"There's something else, Kenna." Evo scrubs his face with his palms.

"What?" I mentally groan. Evo's uncomfortable emotions mean I'm surely not going to like the next topic.

"Ben had done some research on Chris before all this went down. While discovering information on him, and the Gray Pack, he also ran across information on you."

"My parents?" My heart skips a beat and my wolf sits up in attention. She doesn't like my anxiety shortly after I went through a torture session.

"You're from the Gray Pack – the same pack as Chris." His throat bobs.

"Okay. So, I come from a pack that's run like a cult. Got it. What about my parents, Evo?" Though I feel slightly ashamed that I come from the same pack as Chris, I care more about the information on my parents. I want to find them – to know them and talk with them.

He waits for a moment to continue. I can tell he doesn't want to tell me, which is infuriating. If he doesn't want to tell me, I already know I won't like what he says.

"Your mother abandoned you to save your life," he begins. "To save you from the rule of her mate. Her name was Darla Kenner. The pack alpha's name is George Kenner. Your birth name is Skylar Kenner."

Kenner . . . My breath hitches. "But that means –"

 "Chris Kenner was your little brother, baby."

EPILOGUE

Makenna Goldwin

I sit at the edge of my safe haven, watching Bre skip pebbles she'd found on the shore of the pond. The sound of the rock's plunk into the water is soothing. For the last few days of my recovery, I've been uncharacteristically quiet, and out of everyone in the pack, aside from Evo, Bre has been hovering the most. I don't mind – being alone is something I don't want right now. I am grateful for the comfort she provides just by simply existing around me.

Breaking the silence, she asks, "Have you and Evo talked about pups yet?"

I give her a small smile. "A little." And we had. A few days stuck in bed, there was nothing else to do but talk. The discussion of children was a recurring topic. "I'm not ready for it, though. I need time to settle in, first."

In truth, having kids wasn't something I ever saw for myself. It was never an achievable dream for me. But now that I know who and what I am, the idea of having mini Evo's running around my legs is something I find myself imagining. It will happen, but not until I'm ready.

"How are you doing?" she asks after a long pause.

I blow out a breath, continuing to stare at the water. "Numb. My mind is having a hard time processing this."

"You just went through something traumatic." She grunts as she chucks another pebble. "That's to be expected."

I look at her. "That sounds like that's from experience."

Crossing her arms over her bent knees, she nods. "It is. My father was a cruel man. He wasn't afraid to deliver pain as punishment."

I knew that Evo and Bre had a terrible past with their father, but I never knew she had endured physical pain from him. Someday, I hope she'll be able to share those tainted memories with me, if anything but to continue healing from them.

"What do I do from here? How do I cope with this?"

She shrugs. "I have no advice here. Those are demons I'm still working on."

I nod, and then lean my head on her shoulder. "We're going to have to be prepared. My father will likely retaliate once he learns Chris is dead. And if he comes here, it's likely he'll find me. I'm just not ready for that yet. Evo said he doesn't know if my mother is even alive."

"We'll keep it from George as long as possible. If he comes here, he'll have a fight on his hands. We won't let him take you." She wraps an arm around my back and rests her cheek on top of my head. "The Riva Pack has agreed to help, too."

"That's good," I say distractedly.

She squeezes me. "This will get easier over time. Eventually, your mind will heal, and you'll feel a little of the pain each day until eventually, you have it all worked out."

I hope she's right, but I wish it didn't have to take so long. If George is going to go to wage war with our pack, I need my mind to be in the right place. An alpha with issues wouldn't be useful.

Evo has been very patient with me. Even with sex, he's been gentle and reassuring. He took the time to let me think this all through and has been uncharacteristically consolidating. I love him for it, too. This can't be easy for him. With my gift, he can probably feel how little I'm feeling and how shocked my system is. I could feel that it was making him panic, which is why I came out here. There's little I can say to comfort him right now.

I have to trust Bre and her advice. This will soon pass, and I'll be whole again. I have to be. I *will* be. The pack – my people – will make sure of it.

Sometimes, we get dealt what's undeserved and we fall into a dark pit that's inside ourselves. The dark never lasts forever, though. It can't. Because eventually, we learn how to find little pockets of light. The light is my mate and pack. Their light is what will get me through this dark. I just know it.

We hope you have enjoyed A Gifted Curse (The Cloven Pack Series: Book One). Please leave a review to help other readers who may enjoy this series as well. Start Out of the Darkness (The Cloven Pack Series: Book Two) now.

ALSO BY D. FISCHER

| THE CLOVEN PACK SERIES |

| RISE OF THE REALMS SERIES |

| HOWL FOR THE DAMNED SERIES |

|HEAVY LIES THE CROWN SERIES

| NIGHT OF TERROR SERIES |

| GRIM FAIRYTALE COLLECTION |

ABOUT THE AUTHOR

D. Fischer is a mother of two busy boys, a wife to a wonderful and supportive husband, and an owner of two hyper, sock-loving dogs and an attention-seeking fat cat. Together, they live in a quiet little corner of a state that's located in the middle of the great USA.

Follow D. Fischer on Instagram, Facebook, Goodreads, Bookbub, and Email.

DFISCHERAUTHOR.COM

Made in the USA
Coppell, TX
05 December 2020

43170624R00146